This one's for all the buddies who look forward to enjoying that upcoming episode, movie, album, or book together. Some experiences are so much better when shared and discussed with someone who appreciates them, too.

And for my best friend and horror movie partner since 2004, Ashley.
Always looking forward to the next one with you.

PROLOGUE

The echo of my boots against the cement is drowned out by sirens, wailing somewhere close to my apartment complex parking lot. I quicken my pace, past the concrete pillars in the underground parking, toward the exit door. I slam the metal bar down and step into the gray light of late afternoon. The plastic around my fingers is tight. I grasp at the ties of the garbage bags clutched in each of my fists as two police cars screech to a stop before the row of concrete blocks lining the edge of the parking lot up ahead. The sirens stop, too, but the red-and-blue lights flash, lighting up the cars they've parked beside.

What's happening out here?

A small crowd has gathered around the side of the dumpster several feet to my left, along the back of the building. A shallow ditch separates them from the lot. They're all looking into the opening of the small sliding door where I toss my garbage. A woman in a pink peacoat from my floor steps away from the little door—her eyes squeezed shut, her hand pressed against her mouth.

My stomach muscles clench, and I stop at the back of the group as a woman, who's always gardening at the front of the building, and her lanky teen son eagerly step into the place where Pink Coat stood seconds before. Another siren in the distance screeches louder by the second. I glance over my shoulder, toward the entrance to the lot.

A pair of police officers step out of their vehicle and approach the crowd. I turn back to the dumpster. Two men in front of me shuffle to the side and wave the officers over, pointing to the side sliding door ahead. The police don't seem to be in a hurry. I step up behind the mother and son, peering between their shoulders.

Something smooth and pale protrudes from between black and white garbage bags. A pillow? No, there's a waxy sheen to it. Is that skin? It couldn't be. The woman steps aside, pulling her son away, revealing floral material. Pink and blue in some parts —maroon splotches stain others. I recognize that dress. A cold panic washes over me as I struggle to breathe.

Marlena wore that dress the last time I saw her. My skin prickles with goosebumps.

She always flashed me the most beautiful smile when I passed her in the hallway, when I saw her and Scott coming out of their apartment. But I think it was for show.

My boyfriend Logan and I heard everything through the wall that separated us: their shouting, the banging, the bright tinkling of glass. Her crying. And I knew what was behind those sunglasses she always wore—knew about the bruises around her eyes. Every time I heard her cries through the wall, I wished I could hug her or hold her hand. I wanted to tell her she deserved better and that she deserved to feel safe. I wanted to protect her. Even if Logan kept telling me to mind my own business.

You can't save her, Logan's voice echoes in my mind. It's what he said to me after I tried to befriend Marlena one day and ask her out for coffee. I told him that instead of accepting my offer, she'd whispered in a delicate voice like a breeze through bluebells, "If I knock three times, call my mom. Please. Anything else, and he'll kill me." She shoved a piece of paper into my hand and turned away from me after that, ducking into the elevator before I could protest, her pink-and-blue floral dress flowing.

That stained dress barely covers the pale skin of the leg tucked between the garbage bags.

Behind more bags, a hand sticks out toward me— like it's reaching for help. My whole body shivers.

Knock, knock, knock.

Is this my fault? Last Friday night, we'd heard the sound against our shared apartment wall: the knocking.

I called the number, and a woman's voice answered —I guessed Marlena's mom. I told her I heard the knocking. Exactly as Marlena instructed. Logan and I stood by the wall, listening to Marlena cry, waiting for something to happen. Someone else always called the police on them in the past, but that Friday night, when no one came to help, we couldn't just stand by. Logan went to the front doors of the building and called the police. He waited for them down there while I listened at the wall, desperate for help to arrive.

I stare at the dumpster as an officer ushers me to the side. I hear Marlena in my head, the soft croon of her voice, *Call my mom. Anything else, and he'll kill me.*

She'd warned me this would happen. Every shaky breath I draw burns at my lungs. Did this happen because of us? Someone pushes me back into the bigger crowd that's gathered as the officers each shine a flashlight into the sliding door.

The dumpster fades, and suddenly I'm watching through the peephole of my apartment. The police knocked on Scott and Marlena's door, and I remember just waiting—wincing at the loud crash as they broke the door down. In the aftermath, the officers berated us, telling us that the emergency number was for emergencies only, and that they took fake filing seriously since there was no one in their apartment. They gave *us* a warning not to let it happen again. I told them about the deal we'd made when we heard the knocking, but neither of them were interested. They'd left right after.

That was last Friday night, when I still had hope I'd see Marlena again.

Knock, knock, knock.

My vision clears as one of the police officers steps aside and speaks into his radio. The remaining officer shines his flashlight into the dumpster, his beam catching on a yellow circle of flesh around a deep-brown eye. Marlena's dead stare is fixed on me.

Tears slide down my cheeks, burning my eyes. "No. Please, no."

I squint, desperate for a clue that the woman is not, in fact, Marlena. That it's someone else wearing her dress. But I know it's her. We failed her.

"Oh, dear." The woman in the pink coat from my floor steps beside me and tugs at the arm of my coat. "You mustn't look. Come on, now. Let's make room for the officers."

My body goes with the momentum of her tug. I let her lead me back toward the underground parking, the world a blur through my tears. We stop several feet away from the gathering crowd on a patch of grass between the lot and the door to get back inside.

"I think that was that young girl beside you, isn't it?"

I turn to Pink Coat and realize she's staring at me, waiting for an answer.

That young girl beside you.

I press my lips shut. I don't want to say it, because if I say it, it'll make it real.

"That's that girl with those flashy purses," an older man says as he approaches us, stopping next to Pink

Coat. "She's always wearing a new one. And the big sunglasses."

She wore those to hide the bruises, but we all know what was under them. Everyone knew what was happening to her, but it didn't matter. It didn't stop him. My chest heaves as I blink at my tears, trying to stop them from falling.

Pink Coat leans in, shooting us each a wide-eyed glance, and whispers, "She's the one with the abusive boyfriend. I almost called the cops on him last month."

Wait... did she say *almost*? Who else called besides us?

"You don't say." The man glances over his shoulder.

Three officers surround the side opening to the dumpster. Another officer with neon yellow police tape in hand uses his body to make space between the crowd and the line he's creating. They step back bit by bit as he does. A woman with a little terrier on a leash peels away from the crowd and strides toward us with her nose in the air, shaking her head. Pink Coat makes room for her in our circle.

"I got a good look—not that I wanted to. It's Marlena," she says, lifting her dog up into her arms, not bothering to whisper. *Now, it's confirmed. She knew her—knew her name. Maybe they were close. Maybe she had a friend here and wasn't as isolated as she seemed.* "The one with the terrible split lip last summer."

I wince, my stomach muscles clench, and my breath catches in my throat.

Logan and I only moved into the apartment this

summer after six months of dating. We hadn't even been together when Marlena had that split lip. The length of her relationship—the true length of her pain —hits me with an empathetic pang in my own chest. And before us... it's possible that no one had called the abuse in. Maybe they'd all assumed the neighbors closest to the couple would call—the bystander effect. No wonder the police thought we were full of it.

Pink Coat nods. "Yep, I knew it."

Panic swells in my chest. I can't breathe. I glance over at the dumpster. I can't stand here anymore, so I take a step back.

Pink Coat leans in closer to me. "Just terrible. She just wouldn't leave him, even after what he did to her. This is what happens."

"Terrible," the man agrees.

This is what happens?

My chest heaves with anger, my fists clenched in balls. I will myself to take another step away before I lose it on them.

"You poor dear, all that ruckus next door," Pink Coat says to me, then turns to the others. "I heard them all the way down the hall sometimes."

"What kinds of things did you hear?" the man asks.

It takes a moment of silence in the group before I realize everyone's staring at me, waiting.

I can't speak. I can't move. All I can see is Marlena's dead eye, staring at me.

Knock, knock, knock. I imagine it coming from inside the dumpster.

I knocked, Remey. Why didn't you help me?

But I did. I called her mom like she'd asked me to. We even called the police when nothing happened. But we didn't do enough, and it wasn't just Friday... The final actions that led her here happened Saturday night...

"Her boyfriend's been out of work for a while." The woman pets her dog's head, pulling his long hair away from his eyes, and puts him down. The dog shakes and trots toward the direction of the dumpster, only stopping at the resistance from the leash. "That kind of stress can cause people to do some pretty desperate things..."

Knock, knock, knock.

The dog stares at the dumpster. Does he hear it, too?

One officer talks into his radio while another finishes off the line of tape a few feet away, making sure no one can get close enough to see her. I saw enough. I saw too much. All the voices and noises around me fade away.

My knees wobble. Acid bites its way up my throat —I'm going to be sick.

We failed her. I need to tell Logan what's happened.

I stumble back toward the underground parking. I push through the door and step into the dark, damp underbelly of the building. The door closes, shutting out the chatter from the crowds and the static racket from the police radios. In the quiet, I'm left with the knocking, echoing in my mind. A clanging beside me makes me jump, and I look down, only now realizing I'm still carrying my garbage bags. A green beer bottle —one of Logan's—rolls back toward the door.

One of my bags must have broken.

It clinks against the cement pillar behind me. I walk back, slowly, clutching my bags of garbage between my slippery, sweaty fingers.

He put her in with the trash. My body shakes with rage.

This is what happens, they'd said, but it didn't have to end like this. This isn't how it's supposed to be.

I drop my bags and march toward the door. I need to tell the police what I know. They're finally here for Marlena—but it's too late. Scott already killed her and put her in with the garbage.

1

10 DAYS AFTER DISCOVERING MARLENA'S BODY

I long to feel peace beneath the shadows of the golden leaves, clinging to the branches of the trees above me. Children play on the swings at the jungle gym several feet off the path we've stopped along. Dogs chase after each other on the other side of the path, in the soccer field.

Logan seems to be waiting to speak until I give him my full attention, but I watch the dogs nipping at each other's legs and tails.

"When's the last time you had contact with him?" There's tension in Logan's gravelly voice, louder now like he's attempting to command my attention.

The couple approaching, hand in hand, takes my focus instead. I remember when we were as happy as they seem. It was only a few months ago that we rarely ever disagreed, never mind fought.

"Remey, did you hear me?"

"I haven't spoken to Shawn since we broke up." I

hang my head, shuffling to the side to make room for the grinning couple.

My ankle boots clunk against the paved path until I step onto the long grass of the soccer field, swaying in the breeze.

"Nothing? Not even a text?" Logan lumbers to the grass, squinting against the bright sun headed for the horizon.

I stare into his gleaming brown eyes and shake my head no. He frowns slightly, studying me before shoving his hands in his sports jacket pockets. The bright yellow beauty of the sun casts a glow across everything on the field before it sinks into the horizon behind our neighbourhood across the street. It brightens his darker features and shines against the short regrowth of his new buzzcut after the last hockey season ended.

"Then I just don't get it." He shrugs, making a sour expression. "Why are you keeping those pictures in your nightstand?"

I exhale a loud, deep breath as I prepare to recite my reasons again.

"Shawn's family took me to Italy. It was my first time travelling out of the country." I fold my arms across my chest, waiting for his expression to change. When it doesn't, I sigh again and drop the perfunctory tone. "It was a big deal, Logan. It was my first time on a plane—first time travelling out of the country. Just because he's in some of the pictures, you think I should get rid of them?"

He runs his hand over his new short hair and shakes his head. "I definitely don't think you should keep them beside you where you sleep every night. Come on, Remey. You don't see how weird that is?"

Multiple dogs bark to our right—high-pitched yips mixed with low howls of the two hounds, desperately trying to catch up with the rest in the distance. I focus on the road a few meters ahead. The road back to our apartment. I just want to go home, take my sleeping pills, and curl up in bed.

Logan takes a step to the side, so I can't see anything but his muscular frame. "Remey, you always say communication is important in a relationship. So, visiting Europe was important to you. Fine. Can you tell me why you keep the ones of *him*?"

I look up at him, exasperated. "You think I take out the pictures of Shawn and look at them while you're sleeping or something? C'mon, I don't understand what the issue is. I didn't even remember they were in there."

"You keep pictures of your ex—"

"*And* his family. There's only, like, three of Shawn. Would you be happier if I cut him out of them? You want me to ruin the only photos I have, standing in front of the Trevi Fountain, just so you don't get jealous?"

Even if he does—I'm not doing it. I'm keeping them.

He scoffs and shakes his head. "I'm not jealous."

"Then what are you?"

He purses his lips and shakes his head. "Let's go back to the apartment."

So now we're finished talking about it because *he* says we are?

Children laugh on the swings beside us, pumping their legs back and forth, shooting themselves higher and higher into the air with pure momentum.

If I go back to the apartment, he'll swing me back into our normal routine, and because of the momentum, I'll just go with it. It's what I've always done. I've swung back and forth with his moods, hanging on for the ride like those children swinging. Some of them are so little, they can't put their feet down to stop themselves, and sometimes, it feels like I don't have control, either.

I thought I stopped the momentum with that phone call to the police for Marlena. I can't get caught up in it again.

"No." I stand firmly in place. "I'm tired of having this conversation. From where I stand, you're trying to control me by making me feel guilty about something I shouldn't—"

"If you don't come, I'll just go back without you." He glances at the children in the park, and the dog owner walking by, then lowers his voice. "I'm not doing this here."

He started it, and I want to remind him of that, but he takes a few steps toward the road. Always his way.

"Logan." I call his name as a warning—*I'm not swinging your way again*.

I won't just go along with it and be made to feel like I've wronged him. Maybe if he'd approached me about the photos calmly and respectfully, instead of throwing them across the bed toward me, as if it was some big reveal or gotcha moment of betrayal. Logan could be dramatic, passionate, confrontational, and a little unpredictable. If it had been another man, I might have thought he were throwing the pictures *at* me, but no—not Logan. He wanted me to face the apparent secret I'd been keeping from him, literally and figuratively.

He stops and turns back to me. "You've been different lately."

I frown. The cool breeze whips through my long, dark hair, obstructing my view of him. I squeeze my arms at my sides to keep warm. "And you think it's because of *the pictures*?"

"You go for long walks on your own, and you didn't answer your phone when I called you from the locker room after hockey practice this week. You always used to answer me. You used to like when I'd let you know I was finished and on my way home. You used to say it's what made me different from the other guys who waited until they had privacy to be vulnerable with their wives and girlfriends."

"You do that all the time. You go out, don't tell me where you're going, and then get upset when I question you. Don't you see how hypocritical that is?"

He shakes his head no. "It's not the same thing. I

haven't heard you laugh lately. I don't think I've seen you smile in days..."

My eyes widen, and I choke on an incredulous laugh. I brush the hair from my face, tucking it behind my ear, eager to see his expression.

He frowns slightly and leans back, his eyes opening wider.

Has my expression triggered the real reason to finally dawn on him? Is that why he stopped spewing all these odd reasons, even before my reaction? Did the real reason truly escape him? He should be so lucky. I can't escape it.

His stare is blank as he waits for a response. Doesn't he know?

Anger wells up from my core to my chest. It's been ten days. I take a few steps closer to him and lean in. I close the distance between us, but avoid touching him.

"Marlena. Have you forgotten about what happened? I can't stop thinking about her. Have you?"

How could you? Please, tell me you haven't.

He licks his lips, and his chest heaves before he opens his arms and wraps them around me. For a moment, in the comfort of his strong embrace, I'm protected from the cruel wind, and from the awful mistake we made that Saturday night.

Knock, knock, knock.

After the Friday night filled with knocking, the police, and the warning we'd received from them, we'd woken that next morning to the buzzer at our door. When Logan answered, a woman stood there with dark circles under her eyes—Marlena's mother. I told her what happened the previous night and what the police had said.

"Marlena and I had a plan," she'd whispered. "If she knocked, you'd call me, and I'd come over and park on Kingston Road, between the streetlights by the corner. She'd sneak out whenever she could, whenever she was safe, even if it took until sunrise."

Marlena had never shown. I spent the day listening for their return, ready to call her mom again. I didn't hear them, but that very night, it came again—from our shared wall.

Knock, knock, knock.

Logan's arms wrapped around me feel like a cage now. But I don't hear the dogs playing or the children laughing on the playground anymore. I'm trapped with him—trapped in the memory—and all I can hear is what he said that night.

"Babe, I didn't hear anything. They weren't even there when the police came last night. She left. Maybe she left him for good. I hate to say it, Rem, but I think you're hearing things. I think you're scared for her and you're being extra cautious, but you're not being rational anymore. You make up stories for a living. I think your imagination is running away on you."

I'd called her mother again anyway, but the voice-mail was full. I told Logan we should call the police, but he tried to convince me to watch a movie to take my mind off things. Once he realized I wouldn't, I made him go next door with me and knock on their door. When no one answered, he practically herded me back into our apartment and tried to bribe me out of focusing on the knocking with a bad massage. He went to get the massage oil from my nightstand, where he found the photos of my trip with my ex. When he came out of the bedroom, I was already on the phone with the police, but I knew I'd waited too long. I should have called them when I suggested it the first time. They came, and again, no one was in the apartment. That was the last I heard of Marlena.

Standing on the path of the park, the last of the sun dips below the horizon, leaving a golden dusk behind, along with the regrets and guilt I hold from that night.

"We did what we could," Logan's gravelly voice whispers, and any sense of security I feel is blown away like his words, both lost in the wind. "She wouldn't leave him. She had a family that wanted to support her. Her mom was desperate for her to leave and come home, but she wouldn't listen." He pulls away slightly and cradles my face in his big, rough hands. He's staring into my eyes, but I avoid his gaze. "No one could have changed her mind."

He always tries to smooth things over—to excuse away the inexcusable. Right now, it feels good, and I hate admitting it, even to myself.

I shake my head. "She was in danger, and we knew it, and we—"

"Shh." He runs his fingers through my hair, and I hold my breath. It's all I can do to keep from pulling away as he brings my face close to his, his rough hands so familiar, more comforting than his words. "Listen, trust me. I'm messed up about it, too. He left her in the dumpster, like a piece of trash. Like something you just throw away. She didn't deserve that. You *never* should have had to see that..."

I squeeze my eyes shut preemptively to push the image of her dead gaze and outstretched hand away, and end up pushing Logan away, too.

"Scott's dead, Remey. The coward killed himself right after her. He slit his wrists. *That's* who's to blame."

The cold breeze envelops me, and I wrap my arms over my chest. "Logan... I should have... I could have..."

He shakes his head, letting me go, and I press my fingers to my lips before I can say the words—*saved her.*

His face turns sour again. "What you mean to say is it's *my* fault. If that's the real reason you've been acting so different, just say it."

The real reason? He's convinced I'm cheating on him with my ex, Shawn. He thinks I'm using Marlena's death as an excuse for the distance he feels between us. Maybe because I haven't spoken to him—to anyone except my best friend, Nicole—about it since I found her body.

I can't stomach the thought of everything that happened enough to wrap my mind around it fully, and even if I could, even if I knew where to start about expressing my feelings, he doesn't want me to share them. He gets defensive instead of accepting some of the blame.

He wouldn't understand me if I told him I still hear her crying some nights—that high-pitched gasp of breath she used to take when she was hyperventilating.

He'd think I was crazy if he knew I still hear the knocking coming from their wall.

I can't even tell my best friend about it. I can't bring myself to admit it consumes me.

So, I keep it in, along with the memory of the bruises she tried to hide behind makeup and scarves and sunglasses. The thought of how fast my heart would race, walking past her boyfriend after he'd yelled at her. The new necklaces she'd proudly wear— gifts that I'm sure he'd given to apologize for hurting her. The idea that we were right next door when it all happened... when she'd been killed...

I press my whole hand over my mouth as saliva pools beneath my tongue and my stomach heaves.

"You really have nothing to say?" Logan throws his hands in the air and shakes his head, taking a step backwards. "I'm going home. If you won't be honest with me about Shawn, I'm going back, packing my things, and we're done."

He marches toward the road, reaching the sidewalk as I see the black car from the corner of my eye. Too fast. The car is going too fast.

Logan steps off the curb.

"Shawn!" I scream.

It happens all at once, as if in slow motion. Logan turns toward me. The shocked confusion on his face pushes me forward, reaching out toward him. He doesn't see the car. It's going to hit him. My heart fills my throat. The car screeches, swerving around him before driving off.

The relief that he is safe and in one piece instead of lying flat on the road is quickly replaced with a deep, sinking feeling. I connect with the pain filling his eyes.

I called him Shawn. Why did I do that?

"Logan," I stammer, stumbling toward him as the car speeds around the corner, out of sight. I point to it. "I'm sorry—the car—I was trying to warn you, and I don't know why I said that..."

"I think we both know why." He shakes his head, turns back to the road, and looks both ways this time.

"Logan, I'm sorry," I call to him, stopping at the edge of the sidewalk.

He steps over the curb on the other side of the street without looking back. Why did I call him Shawn? Was it because we were just talking about him? I haven't spoken to Shawn—never even thought of him for more than a few seconds—since we broke up after college. We both took writing courses, and I don't even know if he achieved his dream of becoming a journalist.

Logan marches on, his body getting smaller in the distance.

My chest aches, willing him to stop. To come back.

Each step he takes cements the permanence of his decision that feels like the end.

An older woman stops before me, clutching her purse under her arm. "Honey, are you okay?"

Someone's hound dog with long, floppy ears sniffs at my feet.

"Honey?" the older woman asks.

I swallow back my tears.

"I saw what happened." A man's deep voice comes from somewhere behind me. "That was close. You saved him."

Logan disappears around the corner of Kingston Road, in the direction of our apartment, leaving me breathless and alone.

No more swinging in his direction—only mine now —but I don't know where to go.

2

THREE WEEKS AFTER DISCOVERING
MARLENA'S BODY

"She's going to run upstairs," Nicole's voice echoes from her parents' ensuite washroom, attached to their bedroom.

She's only a few feet from the end of the bed I'm curled up on, but she can't see the close-up shot of the actor, peering around the corner while the masked killer stands behind her. I know the whole screen is out of her line of vision, and while I'm impressed by her guess, I'm not shocked. She's usually intuitive about these things, like plots of movies and books. Still, I like to give her a challenge.

"Give her a little more credit," I call back. "She's a scream queen!"

The quilted blanket beneath me offers a soft comfort while I watch the actor on screen turn around and come face to face with the masked killer.

"I'm calling it now." Nicole walks out of the washroom in a black top with a plunging neckline, dark blue jeans that hug her wide hips perfectly, and a glass of white wine in hand. Our "no red wine during horror movies" rule was created after Spillgate, 2009, and has never been broken. "Once the killer comes after her, she'll make a dumb move, like run upstairs or to the basement. Somewhere there's no escape."

She stops by the armchair in the corner, but seems to think better of it and joins me on the bed instead. It jostles me. I take a break from painting my nails a blush pink as she gets situated beside me, both of us facing the screen straight ahead that sits on her parents' dresser. Her vanilla-satsuma perfume overpowers the smell of my polish. She fluffs the pillow behind her head, her curls bouncing with the motion.

"You said *upstairs* originally." I turn to her. "I'm holding you to it, McCown."

"Okay, fine." She smirks and swirls her wine around the glass. "Upstairs, and if I'm wrong, I'll refill your drink for you." She nods to my cider. "And if I'm right..."

I lick my lips, putting on my poker face. "If you're right, I'll do your hair for your big date."

She turns to me with a mock frown and a hint of a smile. "I just did my hair."

"Oh." I feign surprise and embarrassment.

"Ha. Ha." She jabs my side with her finger, and we laugh. She knows my tells. "If I'm right, you have to give that pink polish a rest and try something new for a change!"

"Yeah, yeah. Fine." I grin, examining the remnants

of my pink polish—the same colour I've used for three summers in a row. She has a point.

We turn back to the big screen TV on the dresser, the last of the daylight from the bay window reflecting softly against it. I should close the curtains, but the light on the screen will be gone soon, and I love the view out her parents' bedroom window to the front of the house. A field of sunflowers dances in the wind across the road as far as the eye can see from here, and they almost steal my full attention as the leading lady runs for the front door.

I turn to Nicole and smirk. "Looks like you finally guessed wrong."

She takes a sip of wine and nods toward the screen with a sparkle in her big, green eyes. "Just watch."

The actress tugs at the doorknob, but it doesn't give. With the killer too close behind, she turns and runs across the front foyer, opting to scramble up the winding wooden staircase.

"Have you seen this already?" I eye her proud expression in my periphery.

"Without you? My partner in horror movie crime since 2009?" She teases with a devilish grin. "*Never.*"

Unlike the McCowns' Craftsman-style bungalow, the house in the movie has two stories, and once the scream queen is almost at the top, she slips as the killer closes in. My arm muscles supporting me tense up, and I shift to relieve them, turning to Nicole. She fusses with her tight curls.

"Your hair looks great. You know I was just kidding

about your hair." I twist the nail polish top back on the bottle. "Like I know you *weren't* kidding about my polish. What time's your date again?"

"The movie starts at nine-something. Yours?"

"I'm meeting him at the restaurant at seven." I pause, blowing cool air on my nails, waiting to give my next line a little more attention. "He made *a reservation*."

Logan was never a planner. Far too spontaneous, which gave me anxiety, wondering what was coming next all the time. Mike's initiative is a welcome change.

"I love a man with a plan." She takes another sip of her wine and swallows, grabbing a handful of popcorn from our shared bowl. "I'm so glad you're getting back out there. You waste no time."

I hold up my hands, flashing her my wet nails, and open my mouth.

She tosses in a few kernels of popcorn for me, and I catch them effortlessly. The buttery, salty taste coats my tongue and lips. I finish chewing, licking my lips before I remind her, "It's just a date, Nic."

She sets her wine glass on her nightstand and clutches the popcorn bowl with both hands. "Hey, I know. I'm happy you're giving this guy a chance. From everything you've told me, he already seems way cooler than Logan."

The hot pink streaks across the sky are already fading to a warm orange. A deeper purple hovers above, waiting, like Logan was for me today.

"Speaking of Logan... I ran into him today at the apartment."

"What?" She turns her body toward me, drinking in my statement like she does her first sips of wine—greedily and with full focus, as everyone should. "And you're just telling me this *now*?"

"Well, I think he was waiting there for me. I was collecting the last of my things to bring over here, and he wanted to talk." Nic rolls her eyes as I continue. "You know, he asked where I was staying, and I wouldn't tell him. It was so nice of your parents to think of me and give me the opportunity to house-sit while they're away, and I'm not taking the chance of ruining this peace with his presence. This is my fresh start. Plus, he told me he talked to Shawn, which is just—"

"Shawn?" She balks, pushing the popcorn bowl aside. She grabs the TV remote, and the movie pauses on the frame of the scream queen running into the bathroom. She'll be trapped in there. "Your *ex*, Shawn? College boyfriend, Shawn? The name you accidentally called Logan at the park that day? That Shawn?"

I nod, setting my polish bottle on my nightstand beside my cider and glass nail file. "He said he asked him about us, and of course, he was confused. Shawn told him we haven't spoken in years."

"You already told him that!" She shakes her head and leans back against the pillow pile we created, shoving a handful of popcorn in her mouth.

"Yeah, but guess who he believed?"

Nic rolls her eyes again, tossing up a piece of popcorn and catching it in her mouth. "Typical. But Rem," she says with her mouth full, and then swallows. "You have to stop entertaining him. You're moving on, right? You want to move on?"

I'd hardly call talking to Logan at the old apartment entertaining him, but it's semantics, and I don't want to get into it with her. She wants him out of my life for good, and I understand why. I know I need to move on, but it hasn't been easy to let go of that shared connection.

That day in the park was our last fight. We broke up that night, and though I knew it was the right thing to do, it doesn't make it hurt less.

"I do want to move on. I'm trying—you know I am. When he called the other day, asking if we could meet, I blocked his number."

"I know. I'm proud of you." She nods vigorously, grabbing her wine glass. In the last light of dusk from the bedroom window, I can faintly make out the freckles on her nose and cheeks. "It was a good first step to upholding your boundaries."

"Yeah, but that's why he said he was at the apartment—because he couldn't get ahold of me. A different number called me like five times yesterday, and I didn't recognize it, so I didn't answer. They didn't leave a message, but..."

"You think it was him." She sits up, takes the last sip of wine, and sighs. "I need another drink, but I'm driving to this date, so I can't. Can I get you a refill?"

I shake my head. I'm ordering a ride, but I don't want to show up tipsy. "That wasn't the deal. You won." I nod to the screen where the actor is frozen in the bathroom, terror on her face. "Tell me what you really want for guessing right."

She sets the glass on the nightstand before we share a look. "What I really want is for you to let go of Logan."

"I'm not holding on to him." But I know that's not what she means.

There's this invisible thread that connects us still. A therapist would probably call it a trauma bond after what happened with Marlena, but that's not it. We didn't get through that together. I felt more alone after everything happened, even when he was right by my side. I want to tell Nicole everything about the noises I was hearing at the apartment. I want to tell her that I'm haunted by what I did—and what we failed to do. Maybe she'll understand why she thinks I'm holding on to Logan. It's about more than our relationship. It's about what we experienced.

"Well, he's certainly holding on to you." She shakes her head. "It's just so typical. He's the one who packed his things and left. He's the one who accused you of cheating or whatever, and now, he's hanging around just to see you. He had no other reason to be there."

I push myself to my feet. "He asked to get back together. Actually, he kind of begged."

I grab the glass file and polish, walking to the beautiful, stark-white bathroom, away from the judgmental stare she's giving me, as if *I* was the one to ask *him*. On my left, the boxes I've brought for the bathroom and bedroom sit along the wall in front of the tub and shower.

"Wow," Nicole calls. "Well, I can't say I'm shocked. They *always* come back."

"Hasn't been the case for me." I tuck my nail polish and file into a zip-up case in the box marked Bathroom #1 and pull out my trusty old curling iron.

Shawn never came back. I never heard from him again after we broke up. Neither did Stu, or Jay, or the other Jay. Only two of the boyfriends I'd broken up with tried to hit me up for a booty call or to give things another try.

I pass by the doorway to the opposite side of the bathroom without looking at Nic, stopping before the white counter with double sinks.

"What did you tell him?" There's concern in her tone.

"I told him it's not happening," I call, tucking her mom's curling iron under the sink and plugging in mine, opting for something of a looser curl with my larger barrel.

"Good!"

I lean against the white countertop, inspecting my polish job as the red light flashes, alerting me to wait until my curling iron finishes heating.

This afternoon, Logan had picked up the box it was packed in and asked if he could carry it down to the car for me. I told him I could handle it and took it back, which seemed to aggravate him. He asked if we could get a drink and talk—anywhere I wanted—but I told him no. I didn't let him down gently. He asked where I was going, and I didn't answer. I was busy staring at Marlena and Scott's apartment door. Listening to her sobs. Wondering what happened right before she knocked three times Friday and Saturday night. And when I finally made it to the elevator... it truly felt like if I turned around and got inside, he'd come racing down the hallway after me.

But he didn't. He was still standing there with the same stare—even while the doors were closing—and he never blinked. That's when I realized, it wasn't expectant. He was... fixated.

"It was so weird."

"I bet," Nic calls from the bed. "Like, he was just there? Waiting to beg you to come back to him? Ugh."

"It's not just that," I say, but I doubt it's loud enough for Nicole to hear. I'm not sure it's something I can even verbalize.

She appears in the bathroom doorway and leans her hip against it. "Sorry, I didn't hear you. What did you say?"

I glance at her in the mirror. "It was weird being back there. After..."

"After your next-door neighbour was *murdered*?" She whispers the last word.

I nod and turn my attention to the curling iron, pressing my lips together. Goosebumps crawl across my arms. I turn to the open window by the toilet and think about closing it, but the red light on the curling iron steadies, drawing my attention.

"I really can't imagine what that was like for you. I've never seen a dead body in person before. I won't even look when there's an open casket."

I grab the curling iron and fumble my fingers through my hair, trying to push the image of Marlena's maroon-stained floral dress away. Trying not to think of her pale leg, or her outstretched hand, or the way her dead eye looked at me in terror.

"You don't still blame yourself, do you?"

She knows I think there's more I could have done. She can probably read me as well as she does the movies we watch. But she's never seen a dead body. Could she ever understand what it was like, finding the body of someone you knew—someone who asked you for help?

I set the iron on the counter, turning to her. "I don't really want to talk about it..."

She folds her arms over her chest. "You can't blame yourself. You hear me? She stayed with him. She made the choice to stay. You did the best you could. Even her mom said she couldn't get her to leave him, right?"

A chill shoots across my back as I think about Marlena's poor mother and the circles under her eyes when she came to see us that Saturday morning. She'd sat in her vehicle on Kingston Road that whole night, watching for her daughter, waiting, while she lay dead in a dumpster.

Shivers shoot down my back, and I fold my arms

across my chest, glancing at the open window again. "It wasn't her fault. She was too afraid to leave. I think she tried..."

"And it wasn't your fault either," she says. I walk across the cold, white tile floor and lean over the toilet that sits between the tub and the counter to close the window. "You saw the way he left her, in the dumpster. He was evil, and this is his fault. You never wanted anything to happen—"

My fists clench as my chest heaves. He was terrible—it was terrible, to hear it and feel so helpless. But she asked for help, and I waited too long. I looked to Logan for direction when I should have done what I felt was right. Maybe she'd still be alive.

A lump forms in my throat.

"Remey, I think it's important to remember—"

"I don't want to talk about it right now, okay?" I flip the lock down and return to the counter.

I was too short with her. I shouldn't have done that.

I sigh and glance over my shoulder at her. "I'm sorry—" I grab for the curling iron again, but I miss the handle and grab the hot metal instead.

It bites at my flesh—then burns with white-hot pain. I flinch, letting go, and release a hiss.

"Ah, did it get you?" she asks, wincing.

Instant karma for losing my patience with her. She's the only person in my life who really wants to help. She's the one with the best chance of understanding me. Why am I pushing her away?

I shake my head, but my hand throbs. "I barely felt it."

She inspects me in my peripheral vision in the mirror. I know Nicole. I know her better than she knows the twists she guesses in our movies. She's not finished yet. She wants to feel like I've been fixed.

I turn on the faucet, running the cold water and shoving my burned palm beneath it. It aches at first, and then the pain begins to fade, the icy flow numbing it. She's still watching me from the door in the mirror with a concerned, tight-lipped stare.

What I wouldn't do for a girls' night in right now. I sigh, longing for some quiet time as I turn off the faucet and dry my hands with the towel beside the sink.

"How about I put on some music?" she asks, already scrolling through her phone.

"Sure." I section off a piece of my hair and wind it around the barrel, ignoring the aching pain in my palm. I turn to her and lick my lips before smiling. "I'm just excited we both have dates tonight."

I can make her feel like her support has given me the encouragement I need to focus on the positive. That'll work.

"*And* if they go well," she says, smiling, "I see some double dates in our future."

Worked like a charm.

I nod with the best smile I can muster and release the long strand of curl from the cruel clutches of the hot barrel. Music comes on, one of her current favourite folk-pop songs, and it smooths away what-ever remained of the tension lingering between us.

"I'm so excited." She tucks her phone in the back pocket of her jeans. "And I'm so proud of you for doing this."

"You know the drill. You'll text me when you're home safe?"

She nods and points at me. "You, too. Make sure you text me. I want all the details."

"Same." I set the curling iron down and brush out the curl, grabbing a hair tie instead. My hand aches too much to deal with my hair right now. Maybe my heart does, too. I walk into the bedroom, pass her, and grab my cider, my palm soothed by the cold can. I chug the rest.

"Can I borrow your perfume for tonight?" she calls, disappearing into the bathroom.

"Yeah, it's in the box labelled Bathroom number one!"

My cell phone vibrates against the nightstand on my side of the bed.

"You already smell great, though!" I pick up my phone and almost drop it.

The purple case with lavender flowers painted on it —which Nic gifted me—is slick with butter from our popcorn.

Mike: *Looking forward to seeing you tonight. Are you sure I can't pick you up? It doesn't feel right that I can't make sure you get here safely.*

I smile. Nicole and I have rules. We won't allow our

dates to know where we live until they've made it past a third date. Nicole's will get to visit her house if tonight goes well, but this is my first date with Mike.

I tap the screen to reply and type, *Thank you for the offer, but I'll meet you there. Looking forward to seeing you, too.*

"Rem," Nic says, her voice louder—closer—than I'd anticipated.

I jump and turn. *When did the music stop?*

She stands in the bathroom door, holding out something to me, and my chest constricts. Has she discovered Logan's cologne I kept? I squint at her hand.

No—a folded piece of paper.

I meet her in the middle of the bedroom, between the foot of the bed and the door. Her eyes are wide in frustration, as if she'd been debating whether to hand it over. She passes it to me, and I unfold the lined paper. Has she already read it? It's hard to make out the scratchy handwriting that begins with my name. A letter.

She rests her hands on her hips. "When were you going to tell me about this?"

I frown, shaking my head. "I've never seen this before..."

3

R emey,
 I wanted to tell you this in person, but this letter is my back up plan, stuffed into your bathroom box because I know it's the first one you'll open. I need to tell you how sorry I am. About Shawn, for sure. But I also wasn't their for you after everything happened with Marlena. I didn't know how to talk about it, and I thought you blamed me. You should. You weren't responsible for what happened. I've made mistakes, Rem.

My chest aches for the familiar feeling of being known by someone, romantically, and for the words I wish he'd said weeks ago.

After Marlena, I was scared. I felt guilty. I would have obsessed over what we could have done differently if I believed it would help at all, but I know it won't. And no one else knows what we went through. I don't know what you went through, but I want to. I want to understand you. I want to love you the way I should have. You're the best

*thing that ever happened to me. I don't think I can live
without you.*

My eyes widen in shock. Can't live without me?
He's dramatic, but this is a lot, even by his standards. I
peer at Nicole over the letter. She's watching my reaction, and her stare softens as I turn my focus back to
the letter.

*You're the one for me. Their's no way to change the past,
but their has to be a way to gain your trust back. I'll do
whatever it takes. I love you, Remey. I always will, and I
miss you so damn much.*

Logan

I TAKE A DEEP BREATH, and Nicole and I share a silent
stare with a thousand thoughts passing between us.
Isn't this how it's supposed to be when you love someone? You know them so well that a shared look can tell
you everything you need to know about how they're
feeling and thinking. I can tell she's not as taken aback
by his words as I am. Maybe it's because I can imagine
his voice telling me all of this, and it sounds more
dramatic than anything he's ever said. My chest still
hurts, my jaw clenched. I know I need to release the
tension working up inside me.

Logan had the opportunity to support me. He had
the opportunity to listen to me, and when he chose not
to, I stopped listening to myself, as if his thoughts and
opinions held more validity than mine. *I* made that
decision.

"You know he spells 'there' wrong. Using the wrong 'there' is *so* unattractive." Nicole reaches into her purse on her parents' dresser and pulls out a little matchbook. "Doesn't that bother you—as a writer?"

That's what she decides to focus on? I've known he uses the wrong version of "there" since he stuck a Post-it to the bathroom mirror in our apartment when we moved in together.

Their is no one I'd rather share a bathroom with.

He'd drawn a heart from the steam of his shower and stuck the Post-it in the middle.

I overlooked the mistake in favour of appreciating the romantic gesture. Logan was never much of a planner, so he rarely surprised me on purpose.

Nicole plucks out a wooden match from the book and strikes it against the gritty black side before I realize why she's doing it. She reaches for the letter with the lit match in her other hand, and I pull back instinctively.

"If you keep *that* around, you won't have space for something better. You deserve better, Rem." She presses her lips together. "It's time to let go. You have to let go."

Can I let him go—everything we had—or does he deserve another chance? Do we deserve another chance, now that his walls are down and I've found my voice? Could things be different?

We stand in silence as the flame nears her fingers.

It's one thing to let him go, to ignore him, but to burn this, to reduce the good parts of him that he's finally shown me to ash isn't something I'm willing to do.

She reaches out for the paper, but I make no move to hand it over, scanning the writing again. He doesn't think he can live without me? Was he being serious? Should I be worried?

Nicole's chest finally heaves a sigh, her exhale extinguishing the flame before it burns her. "You've gotta figure this one out for yourself, I guess."

She tosses the matchbook on the dresser between the TV and the door, grabs her purse and empty wine glass, and stalks out of the bedroom. I set the letter on the dresser and follow her. We both walk down the long hallway to the corner of the L-shaped house where she enters the kitchen. She passes the wooden table, walks around the white, marble island countertop, and sets the empty glass into the sink. She stops and leans against it, staring out the window overlooking the back corner lot with the firepit we'd used to roast marshmallows one summer after graduation.

Guilt constricts my chest, making it hard to breathe. I want her to say something—anything to break the tension of her disappointment permeating the room.

She turns, barely glancing at me, then rounds the island again and passes by me into the short hallway. I turn to follow as she reaches the white tile in the front foyer and continues to the door. I follow cautiously.

She opens it to the large, forest-green front lawn. The

sunflowers in the field across the road, lining the deep-purple horizon, wave back and forth in the wind. The bare branches of the huge lilac bushes scattered across the front lawn overlap with the softer small cedars.

She steps outside and my heart lurches. *Isn't she even going to say goodbye?*

She turns to me with a small, forced smile, letting go of the knob. "Don't forget to lock up."

"Nic..."

"Good luck on your date," she says, passing between the two front pillars and descending the concrete steps toward the paved path to the driveway. "Be safe."

She won't look at me again.

I want to call out to her. I want her to come back. I'll tell her I'm not getting back together with Logan again. I'll tell her she was right about him all along. I'll tell her these things because I know it's what she wants to hear and it'll take the anxiety away.

I have to stop doing that. I have to say what I want to say.

"Be safe," I call before she ducks into her car.

I'm not even sure if she heard me. As her car pulls out of the long driveway, I catch something through her windshield. Movement. Is she waving at me? It's too dark to tell by the bottom of the driveway, with the house situated between streetlights on the road. I'm sure it's wishful thinking.

I wave goodbye anyway, just in case.

It still feels like she's looking back in her rearview, watching me.

With my fingertips on the front doorknob, I take one last look after Nicole's car disappearing behind the cedars, reappearing again, and then disappearing behind the trees that line the outskirts of the McCowns' property.

Wind whistles in the darkness beyond. I need to turn on the porch lights. An odd, heavy sensation blankets itself over me—the feeling of being watched hasn't gone away.

I turn back toward the house. From the corner of my eye, a figure strides across the front lawn. A man— emerging from the shadows of the cedars—advances toward me.

4

Panic flutters in my lungs, my chest aching for Nicole to come back.

I clutch the doorknob, slowly pulling it closed, keeping my eye on the man. He's in a navy-blue uniform with a backpack over his shoulder. He doesn't stop at the path. He crosses the driveway and jogs out of sight without even looking at me. Didn't he notice me out here, or did he watch Nicole drive away and assume he was alone? To do what out here? I'm not waiting to find out.

I lock the door behind me and rush across the foyer. I march down the short hallway, into the kitchen, past the wooden table to the back sliding glass door straight ahead, and press the lock down. There's no give—it was already locked.

I take a deep breath, keeping myself hidden behind the curtain pulled to the side of the door as he comes into view. He strides across the back lawn into the path of light from the kitchen, toward the patio by the sliding door. His dark features remind me of Logan's. My heart races. But he's not Logan. He's coming for the door. Is he going to try to break in?

He catches my eye and stops in the middle of the patio, grabbing the strap of his backpack and pulling it off.

"I'm here to read the water meter," he shouts, and removes a clipboard from his bag.

Oh.

I nod slowly, frowning. He takes a step backwards on the patio and scans the length of the back of the house. His eyes widen before his stare focuses on the opposite side of where he entered.

He nods to me and takes a few steps across the patio but stops. "I haven't seen you here before, have I?"

I don't say anything, and he doesn't move.

"Your mom's usually here," he says, still looking at me. He points to his ear. "Sorry, can you hear me through there? I said your mom's usually here."

Does he want me to open the door? No way.

"Did you want me to get her?" I ask, instinctively pretending I'm not alone.

I'm a full-grown adult, and yet, I need to pretend there's another adult in the house to feel safe. To appear protected. Is it crazy, or smart?

"Oh, no." He waves me off, finally cracking a bright white smile. "Not necessary. Have a good one!"

He marches out of sight, and I pass between the

kitchen island and back counter to the corner window Nicole looked out of minutes ago. He's still slightly out of view, but I can see him shuffling from one foot to the other, staring at something at the side of the house.

Something tells me I need to watch him leave to make sure he's gone. What kind of water meter reader works this late? It's almost dark.

He takes a few steps back, and I lean over the sink to keep him in sight. He marks something down on his clipboard and shoves it in his backpack. Without looking in my direction, he starts for the front yard again.

Should I see where he goes next? Am I paranoid? I haven't felt this vulnerable, this scared, since... Marlena.

I shake the thought from my mind and exit the kitchen, turning left down the long hallway toward the bright light emanating from my new bedroom for the time being.

Ducking into the bathroom, I pull my hair up into a smoother, higher ponytail and use one of my ribbons from the Bathroom #2 box to finish off the style. The burn on my hand hurts a little less, but my chest aches from the way things ended with Nicole after finding that letter. She was disappointed in me for not destroying it, but I hadn't even had time to process it yet. She wanted me to go along with her, like I used to go along with Logan. When I don't, I feel guilty. I'm surprised I didn't hand it over to ease that feeling I *knew* would follow because of my decision. It's always easier to swing with the momentum of the people I love.

I walk back into the bedroom, casting a glance at Logan's letter and Nicole's matchbook lying beside it. A McCown family photo catches my eye. Her mom, Theresa, sits in the middle, and both her daughters stand on either side of her. Nicole's older sister, Arissa, shares the same freckles as Nicole, but hers are more pronounced. Their dad, Don, stands in the middle behind them, his chest puffed out proudly, his hands on each of his daughter's shoulders.

It makes me miss my family and the support they offered while we lived nearer. Things would be different right now if my parents and little sister were close by. Kyla would've already invited me to stay with her. It has always been a dream of ours to live together again, and maybe we will someday. But for now, I'm so grateful for this opportunity at the McCowns'. Nicole smiles up at me from the picture as I walk away, back toward the bed.

I unplug my phone from the charger on the night-stand and check the screen, hoping to find a text from her, but there's nothing.

If I don't leave soon, I'll be late for my date. I really wish we could have had a girls' night instead. If Nicole hadn't also had her night booked, I'd have suggested it. Maybe things would have been different. Maybe I'd be feeling safe and comfortable right now instead of jittery, having to put myself out there for the first time again on this date.

My purse sits on the arm of the chair in the corner, and as I go to grab it, I glance at Logan's letter again. Just because I don't want to go on this date, it doesn't mean I'm not over him. I'm not getting back together with him. I don't want to be with someone who'd leave me at a park on my own, crying. I don't want to be with someone who makes me feel like I'm crazy. I don't like this lonely feeling I've had since he left, but to get back together would be a step backwards, to where it's familiar, instead of where I'm about to go—into the unknown.

The folded letter reminds me of my prescription I need filled. I duck back into the bathroom and grab it from the Bathroom #1 box, tucking it into my purse with my cell phone.

I turn to leave, but hesitate, looking back at the window. *Did I lock it? Better check.* I lean against the wall and push against the resistance of the latch. *Locked.*

Outside the small window, I peer around the dark backyard. *What am I expecting to see? The meter reader, out there by the trees?*

I sigh and push off the wall, turning off the bathroom light. On my way out of the bedroom, I cast one last glance at Logan's note. I almost want to fold it up and put it in my purse, too. But why? To read it on my date?

Nicole is right. I need to let go.

I turn off the light, leaving the letter on the dresser.

5

"Do you have a reservation tonight?" The hostess in black dress pants and a black, collared dress shirt glances up from the screen with a welcoming smile.

The main dining room behind her is filled with light chatter, Sinatra heard just above it, and the smell of garlic and onion. Large, modern black chandeliers boast warm white lights at the end of each point, situated close to the ceiling down the middle of the dining room.

I nod. "My date made one. It should be under Mike..."

I realize I don't know his last name as she checks her screen and grabs two menus. "Perfect. Right this way."

She leads me down a long gap between alternating tables for two or four, each set with fresh white plates with burgundy napkins tucked to the right of them and a thick, white, three-wick candle lit in the middle.

She stops at an empty corner booth, and I'm relieved for the space and privacy. Three wicks from the same candle as the other tables flicker in the dim corner with our arrival. I stop at the far side of the booth and remove my gray peacoat, taking a seat on the deep-red material that matches the napkins. She places the menus on the table in the middle, closest to her, and takes a step back.

"Can I get you some water or a drink while you wait?" she asks.

"Water's fine. Thanks so much."

She smiles and leaves, weaving through the dining area.

It's just a date. I'm going to relax and have fun.

If Nicole were here, she'd tell me to order something strong and check the menu to decide what to eat before my date arrives so I really can relax. Instead, I take my cell phone from my purse and use the black screen to check my reflection. My makeup is exactly as I last saw it. The purple case with painted lavender stems from Nic comforts me. Two men at the table closest to mine laugh together, and I tune in to what they're saying.

"... so, if it happens again, give me the signal, and I'll get us out of there," one of them says.

"Oh, I will." The other laughs as he speaks. "You should have warned me your mother's boyfriend gets handsy."

As they continue talking, I remember the signal I used to give Logan when I wanted to leave whatever social event we were at. I'd cross one of my hands over my chest and caress my neck until he noticed. My neck was his favourite part of my body, and the way he kissed it...

The same hostess approaches again, this time with a man trailing further behind her. So far behind, I almost don't recognize it's him.

I'm so used to seeing him on laundry day—in sweats and a hoodie, or at the most, jeans and a T-shirt. Tonight, Mike's wearing a white dress shirt, fitted black dress pants, and a black topcoat that stops right below the knee. He glances at me from behind his signature thick, black-framed eyeglasses. A playful—or maybe nervous—smile grows on his lips.

The hostess steps aside when she reaches the booth, and he removes his topcoat, hanging it on the hook over mine. His face is freshly shaved, too. He cleans up *well*. I run my fingers down the length of my dark brown ponytail, suddenly aware of what I'm wearing, wondering what he's thinking of me. Black tights and a long, satin blouse are dressy enough for the restaurant, but I'm not quite on his level if I compare our outfits.

"Thank you," he tells the hostess, and she nods, stepping aside, her gaze lingering on Mike.

No, not on him. On the red rose in his hand that had been hidden behind her.

"Your server will be right with you," she says to him

before turning to me. "And your water is coming right up."

"Thank you," I say, looking at her but feeling Mike's gaze hasn't left me.

It feels like he's drinking in the sight of me. She leaves, creating space between us, and the vulnerable feeling intensifies. He sidesteps toward me, his shiny dress shoes in perfect condition, and gives me a one-armed hug.

"Hey," he says, his resonant voice beside my ear giving me goosebumps in the best, most unexpected way—a way I haven't felt since Logan and I met. "You look amazing."

I lean forward and wrap an arm over his, my black satin blouse skimming over the cotton of his shirt with ease. His hand slides gently to the middle of my back, sending shivers down my spine. He gives a squeeze around my side, the other toned arm at his side practically bulging out of the white dress shirt he's wearing. As we part, notes of bergamot linger, as deep and rich as his voice. He extends his hand with the flower toward me—a total gentleman.

He grins down at me, and my cheeks grow hot. This is sweeter than I've ever imagined a first date to be.

"I hope this isn't too cheesy..." he mutters, avoiding eye contact.

I take the smooth stem with a smile I can't hide. "No, not at all. It's very sweet. Thank you."

I've never been given a flower on a first date before.

I think he even had the thorns removed. The effort is impressive, but his lack of cockiness in the gesture keeps it from feeling too cliché. He's staring at me with flushed cheeks.

I wonder if he's as tense as I am about dating? Maybe he's feeling apprehensive, too.

A warm confidence grows inside me, feeling less self-conscious at the thought, and I lean in closer to him. He's endearing—disarming even.

I gesture for him to sit, and he scoots into the booth. I set the rose beside my folded napkin as he gets situated directly across from me, folding his hands together on the table before him.

I can't believe he brought me a rose.

"How are you?" His voice cuts through the laughter coming from the men beside us.

"Hungry." I laugh, but I'm serious. Suddenly, I'm hungry, and looking forward to our dinner.

A server brings us our waters and says he'll be back to take our drink orders, and still, Mike hasn't taken his focus off of me. I admit, I've always enjoyed his attention, but tonight feels different. I can tell how much thought he's put into this.

"Want to know a secret?" Mike picks up his menu. "I was only going to pretend to read this while I waited for you, but since you got here first, I'll confess. I scoped it out online before I came. Before I even asked you out, actually."

I smile, opening my menu but maintaining eye contact.

"Oh, you're one of *those people*," I joke, raising a brow to give him a piercing stare before dropping the attitude. "Actually, I usually do it, too. I just haven't had the chance. I moved the last of my things out of the apartment today."

"Ah." He nods, folding his hands together and leaning in toward the table. "You should have asked for help, Neighbour. I guess I can't call you that anymore. Honestly, I'd have been happy to help you bring your things to your vehicle."

We'd only run into each other at the apartment building once after we officially met and he'd asked me out. Of all the possible chance encounters to meet in elevators, the front foyer, or the parking lot, I only saw him those few times in the laundry room.

As fate would have it, I was in the laundry room one night after Logan moved out last week, and Mike came in, asking to borrow some change for the machine. It was the first time we'd spoken. Maybe it was an energy I gave off. All I know is, if he'd chosen to speak to me any time before then and asked for my number, I would have been with Logan, and I would have said no.

"I appreciate the offer to help, but it's... it's been a weird time. It's unusual, moving from one place without really knowing where I'll be next."

I had nowhere else to put my things after the split, so the McCowns were gracious enough to let me store my boxes at their house until I find another place.

"The split." He nods and takes a sip of water. "I get it. You're still looking for a place?"

"I'm staying at my best friend's parents' place until they're back from their trip to Calgary at the end of next month. Just house-sitting while I look for a place I can afford on my own. The cost to rent anywhere in the Greater Toronto Area is just ridiculous. I'll be lucky if I find a one-bedroom for less than two grand."

"It really is crazy out here. How do you like your best friend's parents' place?"

"It's a beautiful house. They have a vegetable garden out back that I get to pick fresh food from anytime I want. It's such a big change, from the apartment to a place with all their land and space. I'm lucky, too, because as a writer, I can work anywhere with Wi-Fi."

He smiles and waits for me to continue. When I don't, he rests his hands on his legs below the tabletop, straightening his posture. "Would you have stayed in the building if you could have afforded it? I mean, not in the same apartment you lived in if you didn't want to, but another one?"

I shake my head no, but make no effort to explain my answer... and every effort to keep the image of Marlena's body from my mind. Her bloody dress, draped over her leg, flashes before my eyes. Mike studies me as I try to ground myself in the present. He must have heard about Marlena's murder. I wonder what he thought about it...

That's what happens, Pink Coat had said so flippantly, but I read between the lines.

That's what she gets.

Did Mike see it that way—as an expected occurrence? I couldn't be with someone like that again.

My phone rings in my purse, and I ignore it, smiling apologetically at Mike until I remember my pact with Nicole. Always on standby for emergency phone calls until the fourth date.

"Sorry," I mutter, and tilt the phone toward me in my purse.

Unknown Number.

Mike clears his throat. "Do you need to take that?"

"Oh, no. Sorry." I pull my hand from my purse and grab the menu again. "Probably a telemarketer. It's just, my best friend is on a date tonight too, so I'm keeping a lookout for her name. Just in case."

We exchange a smile, his seeming to tell me he understands before I turn my attention back to the menu. But I don't want to study the menu. I want to study his face and the way I'm seeing it—him—in a different light. Is it the effort he clearly put in? Am I that superficial that his handsome qualities are assuaging my trepidation about dating so soon again? Or maybe I really am ready for this—to be with someone else... To be with Mike? I can't deny that chemistry I felt when he came in.

I fold my hands in front of me. "So, what do you do for work?"

"I run my own construction company." He smiles modestly.

"Oh, wow. So you're a CEO. Impressive."

He waves his hand, dismissing the notion, and I laugh.

"I have to admit something pretty embarrassing," he says, tapping his phone and turning the screen to face me.

I recognize our latest chain of text messages and frown, looking past the phone at him. I don't get what I'm supposed to be seeing, and he isn't pointing at anything.

"I'm sorry." He laughs, his cheeks flushing. "I forgot to get it, and then, when I saw you again and asked for your number, I felt terrible for not knowing, so I didn't mention it."

Puzzled, I look back at the screen. At the top of the conversation.

Neighbour.

The word is in place of my name as a contact.

"I never told you!" I laugh and shake my head. "It's Remey."

"Well, Remey, I'm changing this contact info right now—" He taps the screen.

"Wait," I interrupt, surprising myself. He looks up at me, his brown eyes bright, filled with candle light, peering just above his black frames. "Maybe... keep it like that."

"Yeah?" He shoots me a sexy grin. "You like it?"

I blush and nod. "It's funny because you told me

yours the first time we officially met. You actually introduced yourself, and I guess I never did. I'm sorry."

He smiles and rests his phone on the table as the server approaches us. "Hello, sorry for the wait. May I start you off with some drinks?"

"I'll have a Manhattan," Mike says and turns to me. "And for the lady..."

"Do you have a Mule?"

"Of course." The server nods. "I'll bring those right away."

"Thank you," Mike and I say in unison as they leave.

We exchange a smile and I look away first, back to the red rose beside my napkin. I run my finger over the thornless stem. "This was so sweet—"

At the same time, he says, "I love ginger."

We laugh, and Mike folds his hands on the table, leaning in. "No, sorry, I was just saying, I feel like I'll be jealous of your drink."

"Well..." I lean in closer. "Maybe I'll share... or... you could always get one next."

Are we flirting? This feels so natural—so nice.

He presses his lips together and leans in even closer, so I can see the detail in his eyes behind his frames. Flecks of warm brown glow by the light of the candle. "I drove, so this will be my one and only. You?"

"I got a ride here, so I could, but I'll stick to one. I've got to go to the store after this and get a few things I'm still missing from—" My phone rings in my purse, interrupting me.

"Are you sure you don't need to get that?" he asks, and there's a hint of tension in his tone.

I glance at him, trying to see if he's more frustrated or concerned. When he smiles, I pick up my phone and look at the same "Unknown Number" on the screen.

What if it's the McCowns? Or maybe Nic, calling from someone else's number? What if it's an emergency?

"Maybe I'd better... I'll just be a moment," I say, scooting out from the table with my phone.

He mutters something.

"Pardon?" I ask.

He shakes his head and smiles, but the wrinkles on his forehead give away his irritation. "Take your time."

I rush down the row between the tables, suddenly wondering what I look like from behind because I feel Mike's eyes on me until I take a right just before the hostess stand and duck down the hallway to the washroom. I can use the time to freshen up a bit before our meal and answer the call.

I press the phone to my ear while I tug the door to the women's bathroom, swinging it open. "Hello?"

"Remey," a man's gravelly voice says. "Don't hang up."

6

"Logan?"

"Rem, I know you don't want to talk, but this isn't about us," Logan says quickly.

He's calling from another number because I blocked his. Wow.

I shuffle into the washroom, clutching my purse, and press the phone to my ear. A strong cherry aroma hits me.

"... realize you don't trust me anymore, and I should have trusted you. I've made mistakes, Rem. I shouldn't have gone behind your back to talk to Shawn."

I slip into the closest stall and close the door behind me, whispering, "No, you shouldn't have, but it doesn't matter anymore. I told you, I'm not doing this—"

I listen for other noises—other people—in the

background of his cell, but I don't hear anything except his voice.

"This isn't about us, and I'll make it quick. I promise."

I sigh and lock my door. "What is it?"

"Today, before I left the apartment—"

"I got your letter." And Nicole was right about it. I'm in a bathroom stall, talking to my ex-boyfriend, while a handsome gentleman waits at the dinner table for me. By hanging onto the old, I'm quite literally depriving myself of the new.

And the new brought me a rose, and he's sweet, and he's interested in me and what I have to say, and he hasn't hurt me. He also hasn't had the chance to, but it's a fresh start.

I'm not getting sucked up into Logan's momentum again. And however difficult it is for me now, I know I can work on it. I need to work on my boundaries.

"I appreciate the apology, Logan, but it doesn't change things for us and... I have to let you go now."

"I ran into Marlena's mom."

I freeze, remembering the look of fear in her eyes when we'd mentioned involving the police. She knew how serious the situation was, but she hadn't agreed with our decision. I wonder how she feels about it—us—now?

"I passed along our condolences to her. She was talking about how the detective is saying Scott killed himself the same night he killed Marlena, and then the landlord came, and she was talking to him. She seemed like she was still in shock. Not that I would have expected happiness... but finding out Scott's dead, getting some closure on what happened... I don't know. Something was off. She was talking to our landlord about the investigation. I think she was looking for something in their old apartment."

Someone flushes the toilet beside me, startling me, and I plug my free ear, lowering my voice. "What was she looking for?"

"I don't know, but she... I overheard the cause of death—Marlena's cause of death."

I stare at the shadow passing across my stall. My muscles tense. "Logan, why are you telling me this?"

"I know you've had a hard time with it, and just, please just listen. I need to tell you what she said. I think you'll feel better." The tap runs, the sound echoing in the washroom, drowning out his voice. "New information... Her mom... so it was a slick..."

"I can't hear you," I hiss, turning to face the toilet, as if a few inches of distance from the sinks will make a difference.

What am I doing, still in here, discussing this with him?

"Her mom said she was stabbed in the chest—her heart. It was a quick death—"

The once pink-and-blue dress, stained with dried blood, flashes before me and knocks the wind out of me. My hand falls from my ear. I imagine the blow, the sharp stab of the blade, and I clutch my hand to my own chest. The blood trickling down her dress, as life drained from her veins and her eyes...

Her dead eye staring back at me.

You let this happen, Remey.

I squeeze my eyes shut, gasping, "Why—why would you think that would make me feel better? That doesn't make it any better—"

"And it was on that Friday night."

"What?" I spin around toward the door of the stall, my heart thudding against my palm, my eyes opening wide.

"The medical examiner or autopsy report or whoever said it was Friday night, and she'd been in that dumpster without anyone seeing until the Monday because of the garbage pick-up—"

"Friday?" I frown. "That isn't possible."

Saturday was the last time I heard her. Saturday, she knocked three times on the wall.

"It's the truth, Remey. Straight from Marlena's mother's mouth—well, really straight from the professionals. Listen, I tried to call you right after I heard, but you blocked me. I had to tell you. I hope it can bring you... I don't know... maybe some peace about the whole thing. We really did everything we could..."

I'm barely listening anymore. I press my hand against the cold, metal stall for support. That Saturday night, it took so long for the police to arrive because of us. They broke down the door again, but no one was in Marlena and Scott's apartment. The officer told us he'd give us a fine next time it happened.

But I know what I heard. And they were there, somewhere close—they must have been. Maybe down in the parking garage, close to the dumpster?

I remember how badly I wanted to call the police again on Saturday night as soon as I heard the knocking. I remember Logan's face when I called the police against his wishes. But her mom says... she was already dead on Saturday? How can that be?

Knock, knock, knock.

I jump, clutching my chest as the tinny echo on my stall door fills the silence in the washroom. I try to speak, but nothing comes out as I open my mouth, my eyes filling with tears.

"Rem?" Logan says my name.

The door jiggles and then stops.

"Oh, sorry." A woman's voice comes from the other side.

"Remey?" Logan says again.

If Marlena was already dead, how did I hear her knocking that night? But... Logan hadn't heard the knocking. That's why he didn't want me to call. He didn't believe me about anything. He said my imagination was running away from me.

Should I believe him? Could this be a ploy to talk? To get back together? He's been acting differently—desperate since we broke up. He found my old college boyfriend and confronted him. He wouldn't take no for an answer after I blocked his number. The way he stared at me by the elevator. Did he call and tell me this just so I'd finally listen? Did he make something up to ease the guilt I feel, and to minimize the damage done by delaying calling for help Saturday night?

It can't be true. Marlena was knocking on Saturday. I heard her.

"Remey?" Logan says again. "I'm sorry. I thought this would help—"

"Don't call me again."

"No, Remey, please. I meant what I said. I can't live without you."

I end the call and take a deep breath, my hand shaking as I tuck my phone back in my purse. I wipe the tears from my eyes with the tips of my fingers. My heart thuds in my chest.

A muffled cry echoes in the washroom.

I freeze. Is that the woman who knocked on my stall? Is she crying? I hold my breath, listening. My body trembles. When no noise follows, I unlock my stall, shoving the door open and gasping for air as I stumble out. I swivel around on the heels of my boots.

All four of the bathroom stall doors hang open. The space by the sinks is empty.

I pace along the openings of the doors and slowly push them open, peering into each stall.

I'm alone.

Turning to the counters, I catch my reflection in the mirror. Mascara stains my cheeks beneath my eyes. I grab a paper towel from the dispenser, wiping at it with my shaky hand as I lean over the sink.

The muffled cry... It must have been a scuffling of

shoes when the last person left... or the door creaking open...

I sniffle, straightening my blouse and inspecting my face. My glossy eyes stare back at me, my cheeks flushed, but otherwise composed. I pull my ribbon tight around my hair elastic and toss my used black, splotchy paper into the garbage.

Into the garbage.

Like Marlena.

7

I weave through the dining room and approach the table. Mike's eyes meet mine, and he tosses the cherry skewer he's playing with back in his thick glass of amber liquid and sets it on the table with a thunk. As I reach the booth, he stands with a grin.

"Sorry about that," I say in a low tone.

His smile fades. "Are you okay, Remey? You look like you've seen a ghost."

No ghost sightings in the bathroom. *But did I hear one?*

I sit down and scoot into the booth when I'd rather stand and pace, working through the new developments to make it make sense.

I put my purse on the booth bench beside me when I'd rather take my phone out and call Nicole. I can tell her now, she was right, and I'd mean it. I just want to hear her voice.

I lick my dry lips and force a smile at Mike when

I'd rather cry. Is that what really happened to you, Marlena? Stabbed in the heart and left in a dumpster for three days? But then, how could I have heard knocking the day after you died?

"Remey?"

I clear my throat of the emotion bubbling and burning all the way up my esophagus. "Just an unexpected interruption. I really am sorry."

He shakes his head. "No need to be. I'm just glad you came back."

He's still shaking his head, looking down at the table now, and I can tell there's more to what he just said. He's genuinely relieved I returned. I wonder if he could sense how close I was to leaving, or if...

I lean in closer, lowering my voice. "Have you been stood up before?"

He picks up the cherry skewer again and stirs his drink with it. "A date left me once. Did the whole 'family emergency call.' You know the one?"

I nod with a sympathetic smile, recalling the deal Nicole and I made to do that for each other if dates turned bad.

He rests his chin in his hand and makes eye contact again. "You know what the real sad part is? I believed her. I followed up with a text, asking if she was okay. Never heard from her again. I worried something terrible had happened until a friend told me about 'ghosting.'" His lips tighten into a forced smile.

My heart hurts for him. Maybe for me, too. Or for...

I take a deep breath, and before I exhale, I can

smell the bergamot from him. I can see the effort he puts into his dates. Maybe he always brings the women a rose. Maybe it's too much—too cheesy—for some people.

"I'm sorry." I try to think of something comforting to say, but I'm not sure what would help. "That's rough."

"Some people just don't have the decency to tell the truth anymore. They don't think it's worth their time, maybe, to just say they aren't interested. To let a person know, so they aren't left hanging. I was really worried about her family member, and I didn't even know what was wrong." He shrugs and shakes his head with a smile, this time a little more relaxed.

"You shouldn't feel bad about being empathetic." I reach my hand out across the table and squeeze his arm. "It's nice that you care so much."

"Well, full disclosure, if anyone in my family called me—really needed me—I'd be leaving my date, too." There's no apology in his tone or expression, but his eyes are warm—passionate, even.

I let go of his hard arm and pick up my copper mug adorned with mint and lime that arrived while I was gone. I bring the mug to my lips, the effervescent ginger bubbles biting at my nose, and take a sip. The cold on my tongue brings me back into the moment somehow, present with the man sitting across from me, studying me from behind his glasses.

"Full disclosure, so would I." If Nicole called, I'd be

there as soon as I could. "And not just for family, but for anyone I love."

"Now that's something, isn't it?" He taps the side of his glasses to straighten them in a manner so endearing, I can't help but smile. "Not only that we'd prioritize our loved ones, but now we've found someone else who would, too." He raises his glass. "To loyalty."

"To loyalty," I repeat. "And to the people we love."

I loved Logan, but he didn't trust me. Maybe I shouldn't have trusted him. He gave me reasons to question him—those times he disappeared and wouldn't answer his phone. The life of an athlete he lived. The fact that he questioned *my fidelity* at the end was so hypocritical.

Mike taps his glass against my copper mug. He takes a sip of his drink, and I do the same. The fragrant mint and lime fill my nose before the zesty ginger coats my tongue again, washing away the remaining thoughts of Logan. Mike takes the skewer and pinches the cherry between his teeth, pulling it off slowly. I watch him chew it with a seeming reverence, without breaking eye contact. He swallows, and I feel the hum of electricity between us.

"Well, Remey"—Mike's deep, low voice reaches me as he cradles his glass in his hands—"for what it's worth, I'd sure hate to miss out on this, but I have to ask, are you okay? You seem off... down. Kinda like the day we met."

We'd met formally so soon after everything with Marlena, and my split, and I still didn't know where I was going to live at that point. It was one of the hardest weeks of my life. I didn't realize he'd seen the sadness in me.

He doesn't deserve this—I shouldn't be here. Not after what Logan just told me. What's the alternative? Go back to a house alone tonight and drive myself crazy trying to come up with an answer to something I'll never understand.

"I'm sorry." I force a smile, shaking my head and trying to come up with an excuse to cut the date short.

"Is it something you want to talk about? I'm a good listener."

Besides the faux pas of talking about your ex on a first date, Logan's call isn't something I can talk about with *anyone*. Logan's the only one who knows what we've been through, like he said. I need time to digest what he told me. Something stirs in my stomach. Not a sickness, but a feeling.

I really shouldn't be here. I take a sip of my drink and clear my throat. "I'm really sorry. I'm just not really feeling like myself tonight."

Mike's chest heaves, and he presses his lips together in an empathetic smile, studying me. "Maybe we should reschedule?"

I graze the tips of my fingers over the rose beside my napkin. "You said people need to tell the truth more. That if they aren't interested in someone, they should just come out and say it instead of abandoning them on a date or leaving them wondering."

He nods, and his expression tightens into a stoic look, his jaw more pronounced, his eyes more focused.

"Well, the truth is, *I am* interested." I smile, and his expression softens slightly. I turn my attention to his gift, to the deep-red petals, then back to him. "I think you're very sweet, and thoughtful, and you deserve to have a date who is present for you. I don't think I'm that person tonight. Actually, I know I can't be."

He taps his knuckles against the table.

Knock, knock, knock.

I wince.

"It's the ex, isn't it?" Mike clears his throat and pushes his glass away. "That was the unknown number. That's who called."

Not a question. Somehow, he knows. In the spirit of honesty, I take a deep breath and nod as he mutters something to himself that sounds like "too good to be true."

"I appreciate your honesty, Remey." He takes a swig of his drink and rests it on the table, pushing it away from him. "Hey, I should have known it was too soon when you told me you were moving after the split. I just—I had to ask you out when I saw you. I had to see you. It was selfish of me to rush you."

He got all dressed up, put in all this thought and effort, and now I've ruined it. He thinks it's his fault. I shake my head no, but he continues.

"Really, I get it. You don't get over someone so easily. You can try. I thought, maybe she wants to try."

His voice softens toward the end as he continues, "Maybe I can help her."

I rest my hand on my purse. "I really appreciate it, and if you're willing, I'd like to try this again."

He stares at the rose beside me and looks back up at me with a twinkle in his eye. "Whenever you're ready, Remey. Since I first saw you, I had a feeling you'd be worth waiting for."

I raise my brow as the server comes. How could he have known I'd be someone worth waiting for?

Mike asks the server for the bill. As the server leaves, I go to take my wallet out.

"No, this is on me," he says, pulling out a few bills from his pocket. "And I know what you're wondering. How could I have known you'd be single?"

It's as if the pressure of trying to keep my composure on the date has melted away, and I can be myself. No pretenses. No force.

This time, I smile, and it's genuine. "No. Actually, I wasn't."

Anyone who heard me talk about Logan, covering for his jealousy or his hot-and-cold moods, could have seen our split coming. Nicole had hoped for it.

It's funny how my perspective changed so soon after we broke up. I realized all the excuses I was making for him were really for myself, because if I had to admit I was with a man who didn't trust me, who liked to control me, and who took his anger out on me, it would have been harder to stay. It would have meant I was weak.

And I wanted to stay so badly because being with him seemed better than being alone. Because he always seemed to know better than me, until the night I heard those knocks.

I know I did, so how could I be so wrong?

"No?" Mike asks with a light huff of laughter. "Then tell me, Remey, what were you thinking just then?"

"I was wondering what you could have seen in me that day you asked me out. It felt like my life was falling apart. I was a mess..."

He shrugs, not seeming to mind that I couldn't finish the thought. He gestures for us to leave. I stand, taking the rose. I lead us out of the restaurant, and he follows behind, past the other patrons, into the cold night air of the parking lot.

"So, I'm still wondering what would have made you think I'd be worth waiting for." My breath puffs out as a cloud. I finish ordering a ride to the pharmacy to fill my prescription and turn to him. "Are you going to tell me?"

"Tell you what?" he asks playfully, taking a step toward me, closing the distance between us at the curb.

My ride is three minutes away.

I tuck my phone in my pocket and focus my attention back to him. "What made you think I was someone worth waiting for that day?"

He pulls each side of the flaps of his topcoat closed over his chest. "I knew you were sad, and I had an idea that whoever hurt you didn't appreciate you. I had a feeling you didn't have the support you

deserved. I wanted a chance to show you something...
better."

"I see." I nod, slightly disappointed his answer
didn't have anything to do with what he saw in me, but
rather the empathy he seemed to feel for my situation.
"My ride will be here in two minutes."

"Then I guess that gives me enough time to tell you
that I hope to see 'Neighbour' show up on my phone
again. Someday." He laughs, rubbing at the back of his
neck. He takes a step away, shoving his hands in his
pockets and avoiding eye contact with me.

I take a moment to smell the rose he brought me.
"Thank you again for this."

He smiles. "I hope you have a good night. Will you
text me when you get back home, so I know you're
safe?"

"It won't be for a bit—I have to make a stop. But I
will," I promise. A black car that matches the plates on
the app pulls up beside the curb. "This is me."

He nods once and opens the door for me. I climb
inside, taking my seat as I stare up at him. A true
gentleman, even when things went south.

"Goodnight."

"Goodnight, Neighbour." His playful tone and
intoxicating scent linger in the car after he closes the
door.

He crosses around the front of the car and strides
across the parking lot. My car pulls away, and
suddenly, I wish I weren't going back to a house to be
alone with my thoughts. I want to be back with Mike,

where I can distract myself from my life. *Which is exactly why you need to go and be by yourself, Remey.* I need to learn how to deal with my own issues.

And I need to try to reconcile what happened that Saturday night with Marlena, because what Logan says doesn't make sense. Could the medical examiner have been wrong about her time of death? Or was Logan right all along? Was I hearing things that night? *The way I was hearing things in the bathroom.*

I don't know why he'd lie to me. Still, it's odd that he called me during my very first date since we broke up. How could he know I was on a date tonight? He'd know if he was watching...

I sink down into my seat, peering out the window at the surrounding cars in the lot. I don't recognize his black car among them. I'm probably being paranoid. It could easily be a coincidence. I check my cell phone for missed calls or messages, willing Nicole's name to appear. When it doesn't, I consider texting her and asking her to come over when she's done with her date. I need to talk to someone, and the only person who understands what I need to discuss is Logan.

I have the power to change that.

I need to tell Nicole about the knocking I hear, and the crying. I need to explain what the guilt and grief are doing to me. I need someone to tell me I'm not crazy or... or to help me if I am before I sink deeper into these feelings and they swallow me whole.

8

Speeding by each of the houses, a mile apart on the McCowns' dead-end road, all the windows are dark. *Everybody's asleep or nobody's home.* That thought intensifies my unease. It's such a dramatic shift, going from living in a place with people on top of each other to a place where you could scream bloody murder and no one would hear you.

We approach the field of sunflowers, shadows standing tall in the moonlight. I rest my hand on my seat belt, ready to hop out and get inside. I need to take off my bra, take my sleeping pills, and get these worries off my mind until I can talk to Nicole.

My driver stops on the road, in the middle of the end of the McCowns' driveway. *He couldn't save me the walk up the driveway?* I climb out of the SUV, grab my little white paper bag and my red rose, along with my purse, and thank him before shutting the door.

I turn around to a dark house, inside and out. I

forgot to turn the lights on for myself.

Really, Remey? Way to end the night.

I walk up the driveway, my ankle boot heels clicking against the pavement as the car does a three-point turn using the driveway. As the headlights flash back down the road in the direction from which we came, I'm left in the darkness. The engine behind me revs and the SUV speeds back down the street.

I stride past the bushes, peering around them to make sure that water meter reader hasn't come back. What a silly thought. *Like he's just going to jump out of the bushes at me with his clipboard and backpack? Come on, Remey.*

There's no light guiding me toward refuge, but something inside me shouts that when I'm inside, I'll be safe. I scurry up the rest of the driveway to the path toward the front steps, slowing by the pillars in front of the door. An odd feeling of déjà vu comes over me as I pass them, and I'm back in the underground parking, walking between the cement pillars. The echo of my boots against the cement drowned out by sirens. The bang of the metal bar on the door as I slammed it. The plastic around my fingers, tight. I clutched those garbage bags in each of my fists as two police cars screeched to a stop. The sirens stopped, too, but the red-and-blue lights flashed. The small crowd gathered around the side of the dumpster, all looking into the opening of the small, sliding door. Marlena's hand, reaching out for help. Reaching out to *knock, knock, knock.*

I stop at the front door, tense with the memory, and glance at the shadows, fussing in my purse to find my keychain. I pull it out, squinting in the dark to decipher which one is for the front door.

Why didn't I turn the outside lights on? Did I really not leave any on inside, either?

The old apartment key is the only gold one on the chain. I linger on it—cold, jagged—before flipping past it to get to the spare the McCowns made for me.

I should get rid of the key—*let it go*, as Nicole says.

A gust of wind blows a smokey, autumn smell through the air and chills descend my spine. I slide the key in the lock and twist it, eager to escape the outside world and the sensation of being watched. I step inside, into the warm reprieve of shelter, and twist the lock behind me. A welcome shiver washes over me with the calm silence of the house, and I set my purse and keys on the sofa table by the door, grabbing my cell phone, the white bag, and the rose. I turn to the large, shadowy foyer.

My first night here, and I didn't think about how weird it would feel to come back to a dark house that isn't mine, alone at night. Those things, I should have known. But I couldn't have known how much I'd wish for the feeling of safety after Logan's call.

Logan sounded so desperate to talk to me—to give me the news. How could he have thought it would make me feel any better? The more I think about it, the more I feel like he was just trying to get me to talk to him. If he was, he'll do it again, even though I told him in no uncertain terms not to call me again.

And what might he say next time? Another lie? *Unless he's not lying.*

I tug my boots off, and the ribbon from my ponytail slips past my shoulder, onto the tile. I grab it before I stand and walk to the kitchen, the cold tile permeating my thin socks. I turn the corner, flick the light on, and round the island counter to the fridge. I set my pills, the ribbon, and the rose on the countertop. A hollow clunking makes me jump, and I swivel around as it echoes, finishing with a little chipping noise coming from the fridge. Just the ice maker.

I open the door and peer in, grabbing a can of fizzy water.

But... huh. *Didn't I leave the kitchen lights on when I left?* It was just after the meter reader left, and I could have sworn...

The hairs on my neck raise, and I twist round quickly, as if I'll catch something behind me that was using the ice-clunking noise as a distraction or taking advantage of its convenient cover.

The kitchen is empty, or at least, I think it is. I could swear I left this kitchen light on. But I couldn't have. I locked all the doors, but someone could have broken in through a window. The bathroom window... I closed it, didn't I? Yes, I closed and locked it. But... how can I be sure? The urge to run down the hallway and check is thwarted by my fear of what could linger in the darkness there.

This isn't me. I'm spiraling. Why am I so nervous—so paranoid?

Because I'm hearing things, a little voice inside me says.

I set the can on the island and step cautiously past it to the wooden table by the opening to the hallway, and grab the back of one of the chairs, staring at the bright foyer. I'm in a new place I've never spent the night at before, and I'm alone. I need to relax. I need to take my pill—

Knock, knock, knock.

I frown ahead at the front door, but my head instinctively tilts toward the living room at the front of the house where the faint, hollow noise came from. That sounded like glass—the front bay window?

I walk through the opening from the kitchen to the living room, between the coffee table and couch, approaching the window with a clear view of the front property. No one stands before it. No shadows linger around, save for the bare branches of the lilac bush and cedars, scattered across the lawn. The branches of a bush tap against the windowpane in the wind.

Tap, tap, tap.

Was that what I heard? It must have been.

But why did it sound like Marlena's knocks—faint but deliberate?

Still, I approach the front window, crossing my arms over my chest, and scan the front property for a vehicle or any sign of someone's presence. With the driveway and road empty, I turn to go back to the kitchen for my pills. I've never needed them more than I do right now. Even that first night after my doctor dispensed a sample, I was more focused on discovering her body. The image of her in the dumpster...

A beam of light catches my eye out front, in the distance. I turn back and lean closer to the window. A steady beam of bright light rolls across the road in the distance. *Is that coming from the sunflower field?* No. The headlights of a car shine brightly as it appears from behind one of the cedars out front on the left. The dark-coloured car creeps down the road going less than twenty, I'm sure. It's dark, but I can't make out the kind. It's too far away.

I press my arms against my chest in an attempt to comfort myself with the realization that they were coming from the left—the dead end. There's nothing else down there.

Could someone have knocked on the window, run across the front lawn, and gotten back in their car hidden in that dead end turn-around? I think I got to the window in time to see them running, but I guess it's possible they'd disappeared by then.

Tap, tap, tap.

The branches tap the glass beside me, and I jump, clutching my hand to my chest.

It *is* possible someone knocked and ran. But why would anyone do that? Maybe it's a teen in the area, bored on a Saturday night.

Saturday night... The last time I heard those knocks from Marlena was a Saturday.

The car disappears behind the front cedars and reappears again. I can make out the colour as it nears the streetlight further down. It's black—for sure. Then it disappears from sight.

Logan's car is black. But I'd have recognized that the first time around, wouldn't I?

I'm taking everything for way more than it's worth, and I'll torture myself if I keep doing this. I need to get some sleep. I walk into the hallway and stride back into the kitchen.

An odd, creaking sound comes from above and I freeze, slowly scanning the ceiling in the hallway just outside the kitchen, where I'm sure the noise originated. I hold my breath, waiting to hear the sound again, but my heartbeat thuds in my ears.

Did I hear it in the first place, or did I imagine it? What I'm really wondering is if I heard the knocking or imagined it.

Your imagination, running away from you.

A creaking comes again from the attic above. Is someone up there? Could that noise just be the house?

I'm not going to investigate like the girl in the movie tonight. It's time to call Nicole.

I walk to the front door slowly and grab my keychain, the cool metal pressing into my hand. I can't stay in here—not with these noises—

Knock, knock, knock.

I jump at the loud noise in front of me.

I didn't imagine that.

Someone's here.

9

It takes all the courage I have to creep toward the eyehole and look through at the dark, empty porch on the other side. I hover my finger over the emergency call button on my cell phone as I flick on the porch lights with my other hand. Nothing. I peer out onto either side. Nothing.

That water meter reader. He was weird, wasn't he? There was something off about him. What if he's lurking? He came out of nowhere the first time. What do I do?

I glance over my shoulder into the house where the attic noise came from and stare at the front door, clenching my keys in my fist. I take a deep breath and open the door, step outside, and close it behind me. I tap Nicole's name on my screen, and as it rings, I glance behind me at the front window, waiting for a shadow to cross it, or some light to reflect against it. The ringing continues, and I realize she's probably still at the movie theatre and likely has it turned off as the voicemail message begins.

"Hi, you've reached Nicole McCown..."

Was it a coincidence the meter reader came right after Nicole left, when I was on my own?

After the beep, I hesitate. "Hey, Nic, I just got back from my date. It was... well... I'll tell you about it when you call me back. Could you call me back soon? I'm feeling a little paranoid. Just hearing noises at the house and... someone knocked on the door." Did they? "I looked right away." Did I? "There wasn't anyone there." Was there? "Just call me back, please."

I end the call and turn back to the house. Minutes ago, it felt like my only safe place. I don't think I can go back inside—not alone. Not with those noises.

I take a step down and sit on the stairs, keeping a wide vantage point of the property lines on either side of the house. The view should give me enough time to get back inside if anyone approaches.

Crickets chirp around me. I start scrolling through my phone, looking for someone to help.

Logan is still a contact—only to make sure I recognize the number I blocked if it ever comes through. Apparently, I don't need that anymore, now that he's found other ways to reach me.

I scroll through to Nic. I already left her a message. She'll get back to me as soon as she can.

I scroll back up to find "McCown" but stop short by a bit, landing on "Mike" instead. Would it be weird if I called Mike? What would I say? I'm scared—come save me. Nope. I don't want him to come over. Never mind the rule—I don't even know him, really, but I don't have anyone else to call, except...

I tap Nicole's mom's name, Theresa, and press the phone to my ear as it rings. They're two hours behind, so they might be finishing dinner.

"Hello?" Her friendly, familiar voice calms me enough to speak.

"Hi, Theresa. I'm sorry to call you at this time—"

"Not at all. Everything okay?"

"Yes, I just keep hearing these noises..."

"Oh, it's Remey," she says to someone else.

The wind tousles my ponytail and small stray hairs surrounding my face blow across it, tickling my skin. I stare out at the cedars and the sunflower field on the other side of the road.

"What are you hearing?"

"Well." I sigh. "There was the ice maker."

"Oh, yep." She laughs. "That still gets me sometimes, too. Especially if I'm right beside it."

"Mhmm, oh, I was." I start to laugh, a bit forced at first, but then she's laughing too. I take a deep breath, shaking my head. "Then, there was this creaking upstairs."

"Just above the kitchen?" she asks.

I straighten. "Yes, how did you know?"

"That's the furnace. When it turns on and off, the ducts up there jiggle, and the floor's so old, it creaks. It'll happen anytime the heat comes on."

And the heat *is* on.

"Ah, okay, it just sounded like..."

"Like someone walking up there?" There's amusement in her tone. "I know. Don will tell you, that got to me too, at first. Then, there's the whistling noise. That happens when it's windy out near the window in the bedroom. We need to get new ones installed soon. There's also a hissing sound that comes from our water heater in the basement. That's all I can think of for now, but Remey, I'm sure it's fine. And Karla and Richard up the road will surely stroll down to take a look if you need them. I'll text you their contact info."

"Oh, thank you." I turn back to the house, and suddenly it feels safer than being out here, alone in the cold. "Thank you, Theresa."

"Is Nic available for a sleepover? Maybe she could come and keep you company tonight?"

"She's busy tonight, but I know she'll call me when she's free."

"Okay, great. In the meantime, if you're nervous, I like to put the TV on in our room. It drowns out the other noises."

"Thanks so much. Hope you and Don are having a great time."

"We are. Thanks again for watching the house. I'm here if you need anything else."

"Have a good night."

"Goodnight, Remey."

I end the call and turn back to the house. Light glows inside the front bay window from the foyer. The noises here are normal. It's me who turns them into something insidious and threatening. After what I experienced at the apartment, maybe it's even normal for me to be acting this way. I need to get to the bedroom, make sure I'm alone in there, and then I can try to relax with a movie—just not a scary one.

I step inside and lock the door behind me again, lingering in the middle of the foyer. I take a deep breath and revert back to my childhood self as I rush down the hallway, past the kitchen, and make a break for the bedroom. With each open, shadowy doorway I pass, my muscles clench until I reach the room at the end of the hallway.

I swivel around and close the door behind me, flicking the light switch on.

Better already. Time to make sure I'm alone.

I catch my breath as I check in the closet behind the clothes and in the bathroom behind the shower curtain. My cell phone vibrates—Theresa sending me the neighbour's number. The bathroom window is closed and locked, just as I remembered. I cross the bathroom again, deciding to check under the bed, which is far too low for anyone to slide under... or is it?

Out of my peripheral vision, I catch something on the white bathroom counter. My curling iron. It's plugged in with the steadily glowing red light on the handle.

I didn't leave it that way... did I? Does it have an automatic shut-off if I had? Maybe that's only on new models. I've had this one since college... It burnt my hand earlier tonight, and then I opted to put my hair up. I wouldn't have left it on... But I have before.

I press the button to turn it off, and the small burn mark on my palm suddenly aches as a reminder of my absentmindedness and the harm it could cause. This house could have burnt down.

I double-check under the bed before I sit on it and gather my bearings.

Theresa told me about all the noises she could remember, but I still wait, listening for another that seems close. The wind lightly whistles through the cracks in the bedroom window, just like she said it would. Other than that, all I can hear is the faint sound of my heartbeat in my ears that slowly disappears as I relax.

My phone vibrates in my hand, and I jump, checking the screen.

Not Theresa. Not Nic.

Mike: *Home safe?*

Ugh, I forgot to message him.

Home safe. Thank you for the drink. I send the message and change into my satin pajama set, still listening for any noises. Any knocking.

My phone vibrates on the nightstand, but I don't jump. I sit on the comfy quilted blanket and grab my phone.

Mike: *I'm only asking this because you seemed so different after taking that call. Are you sure you're okay?*

I take a deep breath and type, *It's just been a rough few weeks, and I appreciate you understanding tonight.*

Mike: *Of course. Here if you need me. You looked amazing tonight and you have the most beautiful smile. I hope you're smiling again soon.*

I grin, setting the phone on the nightstand. While I hope that the next alert is from Nic, it wouldn't hurt to occupy myself with a Mike text-exchange until she's available. I swing my legs into bed and pull the covers up to my neck, glancing over at the TV remote and the remnants of the bowl of popcorn on the nightstand on Nicole's side of the bed. If I turn on the TV, maybe I'll relax enough to sleep...

Sleep. I forgot my pills in the kitchen. Groaning, I push myself to sit up and hop off the bed, walking toward the door. I open it to the bright hallway and shuffle to the kitchen, past the table, and as I reach for the white bag, I notice it's the only thing on the island countertop. *Where did the rose go?*

My phone vibrates against the nightstand, over and over. I can hear it from here. I rush back down the long hallway, the ringing getting louder. I swing the door closed behind me and hurry to the nightstand.

"Unknown Number" glows on the screen. Panic swells in my chest as I take a step back from the phone.

Logan. Of course it's him. He never listens to me. He always did whatever he wanted, and now that we've broken up, he still thinks he can.

I grab my phone and jump back into bed, tugging the blanket up to my chest. The phone stops ringing, but I watch the screen, ready for it to vibrate in my hand again.

Logan won't believe something unless he wants to. He must still believe that I want to talk to him...

About Marlena? Or reconciling?

I don't want either. I don't want to talk about her. I don't want to think about her. I wish I could go back and do more for her. I could have done more. And I don't want to think about Logan, either.

Why won't Logan just leave me alone? Why is he torturing me?

But it's Nicole's voice that answers: *Because you haven't let go. You need to cut him off completely.*

I clutch the phone to my chest and close my eyes. The whistling breeze slips around the windowsill, and with my head pressed to the pillow, my heartbeat is back in my ear, filling my head.

Please don't let him call again. Please let me find peace with Marlena. Please, no more knocking. I tried to help you, Marlena, I promise I did.

But I know I could have done better.

10

K*nock, knock, knock.*

I shoot upright in bed, gasping for breath, scanning the surrounding darkness. I must have fallen asleep. How? I didn't take my pills, did I? I haven't slept without my pills since they were prescribed to me two weeks ago.

Marlena was dead when I heard those three knocks the second night. I was sure I'd heard them before Logan's call, but now, what if it's all in my head? What if I'll always hear the knocking? What if it's my conscience? What if it's because I know deep down, I could have done more—should have done more.

My heart thuds in my ears as I shove off the quilted blanket. I shiver; my body, once hot and sweaty beneath the blanket, now cold in the air. And my head feels foggy—the same feeling I get after taking my pills and waking up too soon after.

Knock, knock, knock.

I jump, clutching my hand to my satin shirt against my chest.

That was real. Was that the front door? That has to be real or I'm losing my mind. I reach for the lamp and flick it on, squinting at the light and peering through the empty room, looking for my phone. A sharp pain pulses in my head, a reaction to the light, maybe. I sweep my hand along the empty nightstand. I must have fallen asleep with it in my hand. I scour the bed linens beneath me, constantly glancing back up at the door.

How? How is this happening when Marlena and her boyfriend are dead?

No one else knew about the knocking except Marlena's mom, the police, and...

Logan. Logan is the only other person who knows what those knocks meant. He knows we failed her. Does he know where I am right now? If so, he must have followed me. Why would he be doing this? To scare me. To terrify me enough—make me question myself enough—to make me reach out for help.

Where the hell is my phone? I have to get out of here.

I stumble to the window and look outside into the black beyond. No cars in the driveway. No movement —save for the dancing shadows of sunflowers across the road. I rest my hand against the window frame, my legs and arms weak and heavy. I shuffle to the bed and drop to the carpet, looking under it into the wide-open space. My phone has to be here somewhere.

I push myself to stand, almost tripping, and stagger toward the door.

No more knocking.

No other noises.

I drop to the ground again and press the side of my face against the rough, dry carpet as hard as I pressed it to the cold wall between our apartments. I listened for Marlena then. I watch for shadows now.

Nothing. Just a clear view of the hallway floor ahead. I roll over, not wanting to get up, not feeling like I have the strength, and scan the floor for my phone while I'm down here. I have to get up. I have to find my phone. I push myself up, stop at the end of the bed, and rip the quilted blanket off, shaking it and tossing it to the floor. The sheets come easier. I throw off the pillows, panting as the room seems to spin around slowly.

Marlena's dead stare flashes through my mind. What must have gone on in their apartment, behind that wall, to have made her knock? It won't stop. The knocking won't stop, and now, I might not be alone here. This is a nightmare. I'm living a nightmare.

My phone's not here. Is this really happening?

I stumble into the bathroom and flick on the light. The bright white helps me regain focus. I rummage through the Bathroom #1 box, my head still dizzy. I grab my glass nail file—the closest thing I have to a weapon—gripping it with all my strength as I stagger out of the washroom and focus on purposeful strides to the door.

If Nic came and found me like this, she'd try to ground me in reality—but it's her reality—and mine has become painted with paranoia.

If it's Logan, if he's really pulling this shit to make me call him for help, this might be the way to do it. Maybe he's making sure I can't call the police right now. He wouldn't hurt me—I'm almost sure of it.

Another part of me, deep down, wonders that if it's not Logan, why should I leave the only place that seems safe?

But if someone were to come in, I'd be trapped in here with the bay window.

I have to get somewhere safe. Maybe to the closest neighbours, to Karla and Richard.

I hold the glass file at my side and open the door slowly. It releases a short, high-pitched creak. If someone's here, they know I'm coming out. My burst of nervous energy forces me down the hallway, both of my hands held up at my sides as I stagger past each door. A chill breezes over my neck, damp with sweat. My muscles tense, ready for whatever lies at the end— by the door in the kitchen—and beyond.

Just before the kitchen, I see something on the tile floor in the doorway. Something dark, scattered. I slow down enough to register red spots—petals? A trail of red rose petals is scattered along the white tile, past the kitchen table, and right out the open sliding glass door. The curtains on each side blow in the wind, sending shivers across my whole body with a sobering effect.

Those rose petals... There are so many. More along

the trail than just the rose Mike gave me would have created.

I might have been wrong about the sounds. Maybe I was wrong about leaving the lights on. But I didn't leave the sliding door open, and those petals—all those blood-red petals...

I'm not alone.

11

___

I take one last look over my shoulder at the flowing curtains as I round the corner and make a break for the front door. The cold wind sends goosebumps across my exposed skin. I bend to grab my boots, throwing off my equilibrium. Righting myself, I reach for the doorknob, ready for someone to stop me, or for the knob not to twist, like in the movie. But it does. As I pull, the door flies open, and I steady myself by letting go.

I expect to see Logan standing on the porch or at the bottom of the steps, waiting for me.

No one stands on the other side. My path to the road seems clear.

I jump down the front porch steps and break into a run at the path, across the front lawn. The freshly cut grass tickles my bare feet. I sprint toward the street. My muscles clench, and I tighten my grip on my boots as I pass the place the water meter reader seemed to appear from, behind the front cedar bushes.

I glance to my left. Nothing.

To my right. No movement in the shadows.

It's a clear break for the dark road ahead. Once I reach it, I look back at the house. It rocks back and forth in soft focus before my hazy vision.

I hop on one leg, pulling on a boot, gasping for oxygen. I almost fall as I struggle to push my foot into the next one.

This is it, Remey. You got out of the house. Take a breath and get it right.

I inhale the smell of burnt leaves in the autumn night. The cold air burns my lungs as I break into a run again. My boots crunch over the gravel, kicking up the little stones behind me as I go.

Whistling winds bend the tree branches on either side of the road and the sunflowers dance in the moonlight. Light ahead. A streetlight. I pass beneath it, fixing my eyes on the distant landscape, desperate for the closest neighbour's house to come into view. I squint through the stray hair blowing across my face, desperate to see the house in the obscurity of shadows before my eyes. Something on the side of the road catches my eye first. Something I recognize on the shoulder of the road. Logan's car.

It's him.

Is that why he let me get away? Was this his plan all along—to be here, waiting to rescue me? Or to do something else?

My arms hang heavily at my sides as I clench the glass nail file in my fist, checking over my shoulder. The dark, isolated road lies behind me. I can't see the McCowns' anymore. I look ahead at the car facing me. A figure sits in the driver's seat, his car facing the opposite way as if he'd been driving on the wrong side.

He's waiting for me. He wanted me to come out. He wanted me to come to him.

I slow to an unsteady wobble of a walk, panting. I approach the car, parked between the streetlights. A little yellow light glows over the distant hill. The neighbours' house comes into view. I stumble closer, but I'm focused on Logan's shadow. He watches me right back.

"Logan?" I shout, gasping for breath as my boots clomp against the pavement. "Why are you doing this?"

I near the hood of the car, shuffling off of the gravel on the side of the road. My boots slip easily over the dewy grass. My hand glides along the side of his car for balance.

I step on something hard, sucking in a sharp breath. I lift my foot and lean against the car. A shard of green glass sticks out from the sole of my boot. A broken beer bottle?

"Logan," I hiss. "What's going—"

He stares out the front window, his wide eyes avoiding me. *Why is he sitting like that?*

I take a step closer, despite my fear he'll jump at

me, because something isn't right. I peer into his open window. I still can't see.

My fingers feel beneath the ledge of the car door handle and I pull, opening it. The interior light shines bright. I squint through it.

Blood trickles from the gashes in both of his wrists.

No, no, no. This isn't happening.

My stomach clenches. His right hand holds a thin, bloody shard of green glass wrapped in ribbon... my ribbon, lying in his lap. Blood pools in his lap against his light jeans, soaking them. My wide eyes search in shock, my stomach heaving. I reach in toward him, and a blood-curdling scream slices through the night.

It's me. I'm screaming.

"Logan," I shriek.

His arm is cold against my fingers. His cheek, too.

What if he's dead? He is—he is dead. But if he did this—if he killed himself—I can't talk to him ever again. But I have to. I need to. This can't...

My stomach heaves with pain, wave after wave. How could he do this? How did this happen? Is this really happening?

"Help! Somebody—" But there's no one out here. I was yelling, I know I was, and no one showed up. Are the neighbours too far to hear me? The light glowing from the upstairs window at Karla and Richard's taunts me.

I turn back to Logan, resting my weight against his car door, my eyes searching for material, something to stop the bleeding.

His phone is in his other hand, the screen shattered, the purple case—cracked.

I take a second look at the bloody purple case. The painted lavender flowers.

Not his phone. Mine.

He was in the house. He took my phone.

I grab it from his hand and tap the screen, but it remains black. I push the button on the side and wait. Still black.

Something red catches my eye, not where he sits, but on the passenger side window.

I'm sorry, written in blood. The words hit me like the metallic scent, overpowering every other sense.

I drop the broken phone and stumble, pulling my head out of the car, gasping for fresh air. The cold night fills my lungs and hits the tears in my eyes, blurring my vision until the world is a deep, dark sea of pain. My stomach churns, and a hard lump forms in my throat. Gravel crunches beneath my boots until they echo against the asphalt. I stagger to the center of the road, gasping for air.

Logan's dead.

Each step I take, imbalanced by the glass in the sole of my boot, threatens to send me tumbling to the ground. I'm heavy—all my limbs are so heavy.

Logan's dead, and I can't see straight. I have to reach the neighbours' house. I need help. The neighbours... Why can't they hear me? Were these Marlena's final thoughts?

"Help," I say.

The world turns black.

12

My eyes flutter open to darkness, my head aching. A hand comes into focus. A hand setting a bottle of water on the table in front of me. A pillow props my head up, and I rub my cheek against it. Not soft, like I imagined. Not the bed. I'm on the couch—Nicole's parents' living room couch.

Heavy footsteps fall away from me, softer as they leave the room.

"Nicole?" I call.

Come back, Nicole.

I open my eyes wide, staring into the dim living room. Warm light cascades in from the hallway. My head throbs. I reach for the bottle, my arm trembling, my limbs still heavy.

"Remey?" A deep voice comes from the kitchen and footsteps follow, coming closer again.

Logan?

No.

All at once, images flash through my mind of Logan in his car, his wrists slit. The bloody shard of green glass. Logan's letter to me, telling me he couldn't live without me. My ribbon wrapped around one hand with the shard of glass and my phone in his other hand —his bloody hand.

Someone's walking toward me, their shadow backlit by the hallway light.

Not Logan. Logan's dead—unless that was a dream. Oh, please, please, please, I'd give anything for it to be a bad dream.

Panic struggles in my chest like a caged bird as my vision comes into focus.

Mike crouches beside the couch with a concerned expression on his face. He studies me intensely from behind his thick-framed glasses.

"Mike?" I whisper, craning my neck away from him. He's still wearing his white, collared dress shirt and black dress pants. "What are you doing here? How—"

"You called me." Whatever expression I make must show my confusion, because he frowns. "You don't remember?"

"No," I say, my lips and tongue so dry.

"You stopped answering my texts, and even though you told me you were okay, I couldn't shake the feeling something was wrong. Then you called and asked for help. I just want you to rest up and have some water."

I shake my head. He pushes the bottle closer to me.

"How did you find me?"

"I found you on the road, Remey. I almost hit you. I

kept calling your phone, hoping you'd answer. I was kind of distracted, and then there you were, out there on the road alone. The police are on the way. Do you remember what happened?"

"I think so. I woke up, and I felt so disoriented. I thought someone was in the house, and then there were rose petals... leading to the backyard."

He nods. "I saw those when I brought you in. Both the front and back doors were wide open. I didn't understand... I mean, I didn't know why you'd have torn up the rose I got you... but now it makes sense."

"*That* makes sense to you?"

He shifts to sit on the edge of the coffee table in front of me. "It's your ex. It was the phone call you took during our date that changed everything—your whole demeanor. I think he's stalking you, Remey. I think he followed you to our date. I'd even bet he interrupted it on purpose, and then followed you back here. Maybe he brought you flowers. Maybe he was hoping to win you back, and he saw the rose from me..."

As he says it, I imagine it all. Logan watching us from the restaurant window. I thought I'd felt him there in the parking lot, but I couldn't see him. I shiver, hugging my arms against my chest, recalling the urge to scan the dark parking lot.

What if he was following me? If he followed me to the drug store, he knows I picked up my pills. He's the one who suggested I start taking them.

Could he have drugged me somehow in my sleep with my pills? How could he have done it otherwise? I got some fizzy water from the fridge, but I never drank it. I haven't drank anything since I returned.

"My pills..." I blurt. "Did he drug me?"

Mike frowns. "He drugged you? Wow, he could have, I guess. How? What pills?"

I rub at the sharp pain in my temples and notice the cuff of an unfamiliar sweater on me. I feel like I'm in someone else's body—that this is all happening to someone else.

He lifts his chin, nodding to the blue sweater I'm wearing. "I had it in my car. I put it on you once I brought you inside. You seemed so cold." He carried me inside, put a sweater on me, and watched over me until I woke. It's so much effort from someone I barely know, and I don't know how to process it. "Sorry, you said *pills*?"

I lick my dry lips and nod. "Yeah, could you get me my pills? They're in the kitchen. In the white bag on the counter."

If I didn't take any, they won't be open yet.

"Of course. Hold on." He stands. "Remey, if you've been drugged, they'll be able to test you to find out what you were given..."

He disappears into the kitchen.

Why? Why would Logan do all this and then kill himself? My stomach heaves again, and I press my hands against it. Mike's so calm—too calm. He doesn't realize what's happening.

Logan killed himself after all his failed attempts to connect with me.

"I saw Logan… on the road. He's dead, Mike," I call to him, desperate to impress the gravity of the situation on him. This is an emergency. He needs to understand what's happened to Logan—to me. *I* need to understand it, and maybe he can help. "Do you hear me?"

I struggle to sit straighter, leaning back against the stiff pillow.

"What?" He re-emerges with my bag.

"My ex. Didn't you see him—his car—when you found me?" I take the white bag from him and grab my pills from inside. It's still sealed.

He frowns and crouches down beside me again. "I found you in front of *this house*, Remey."

"Wait… what? *Here?*"

He nods. Confusion clouds his stare as he tilts his head to the side and frowns.

How? I must have passed out and then came to. I must have been in and out of it, trying to get back here —to do whatever it took to get help. Maybe I even crawled, but my hands and knees don't hurt.

"I found you at the bottom of the driveway, just passed out. I didn't understand how. You only had one drink at the restaurant. And I knew you must have been unconscious because it was so cold… You were so cold."

I rub my dry eyes and stare down at the white bag in my lap. "I don't think he used my pills… but I feel so out of it. I—you said the police are on their way?"

He nods, his eyes wide as he stares at me. "I don't

know what Logan did to you, but you need to tell the police everything you know."

"I just—I can't believe he'd do this. And I can't believe you were here... to help me... Did you see a car on the shoulder of the road on your way in?"

He frowns and looks up to the right. "I was pretty distracted, trying to call you, but now that you mention it, I think I remember seeing a car parked. Yeah."

"That's him—*was* him. It was so... it was terrifying, Mike." My voice trembles, and I pull my hands up into the sleeves of Mike's sweater for warmth. "Discovering him like that..."

Imagining Logan—his body sitting there in his car. He had this dead stare, but unlike Marlena's, from a distance, it looked like he was still alive and awake. Their dead eyes stare at me, cold and accusatory. I found them when it was too late. They stare into my soul. They see who I really am.

"I never wanted to—I never wanted it to happen again." I gasp for breath and pull Mike's sweater away from my chest to try to catch it. "I can't... keep doing it."

My whole body convulses, adrenaline pulsing through my veins with no place to escape. My muscles clench. My body rocks back and forth.

"Can't keep doing what?" He wraps his arms around me, but he pulls his face away to look into my eyes. "You're shaking."

I can't keep discovering dead people.

He gives me a long hug, and with his warmth, I'm able to stop shaking. When he releases me, pulling his phone from his pocket, he leaves one hand remaining on my leg. "I called the police about ten minutes ago. I know we're on the outskirts of town here, but it shouldn't be too long. I told them it was a possible break-in with the front door open. I told them to send paramedics, too. When I saw you on the road, I didn't know what to make of it—"

"I don't, either. I don't... understand..."

He stands, my leg chilled by the absence of his warm hand. "I'm going to make you a hot tea."

His kindness is the only thing grounding me in reality right now—in the possibility that I'll get through this.

"Thank you." I squint up at him, still shivering.

He nods, his concerned expression softening only slightly, as if he's considering staying with me, before he leaves the room.

Seconds later, a far-away whooshing sound comes from the kitchen as the faucet starts running.

I don't understand why Logan would do all this... I still can't believe it.

His letter said he was feeling some of the same things I've been feeling. Guilt. Did he feel so guilty that he couldn't stand it? Did I make him feel so alone in this that he couldn't take it? His letter said he couldn't live without me.

Tears burn my eyes. He was here. We were so close, and I made him feel like he couldn't reach out for help. Pain shreds through the depths of my spirit, and I squeeze my eyes shut, wrapping my arms around me.

He'd written "I'm sorry" in his own blood on the car window. The guilt—he was filled with it like me.

And in his last moments on earth, I shunned him. He saw me moving on with someone else. And it killed him.

I picture Logan in my mind's eye, standing in front of the McCowns' with a bouquet of roses, like Mike suggested. Tears spill down my cheeks.

The roses.

All those petals, ripped off...

I open my eyes, still alone on the couch.

If Mike is right, Logan's trail of petals was leading me into the backyard. What if I'd taken that path? What was he trying to show me in his final hour before walking back to his car and slitting his wrists?

I push the blanket off me, shivering with a combination of chills and adrenaline. I grab my pills and shove them in the pocket of the sweater—Mike's sweater. What would I do without him here? I take the water bottle and stumble down the hallway, into the kitchen.

Mike turns and looks over his shoulder by the stove, holding the kettle with a concerned stare. "You should be lying down until the police get here. The medics will need to check—"

"I can't, Mike." I lick my dry lips and twist open the bottle of water. "I don't understand what's going on. I need to make sense of it."

I walk to where the rose petals meet the now closed sliding glass door and stare out into the night. The trail is all but dissipated, all the petals blown away like clues to the answers I need. A small fire crackles in the pit at the back, by the tree line.

"Do you see that?" I point to it.

You need to let this go.

Nicole's words echo in my mind. I slide the door open and the cold night air washes the sluggish brain fog away. Quivering, waking from my stupor, I set my water bottle down on the table and hug Mike's sweater against my chest, watching the orange flames before the trees beyond.

That's where the trail leads.

Once the police get here, whatever's out there will become evidence. I won't be able to see it for myself. I need to know.

I step outside.

13

Nicole's parents' firepit crackles, the flames biting at the night air above.

There's barely a path to follow anymore. The wind teases the remaining rose petals, and I wouldn't be sure which direction to walk in anymore, if it weren't for the fire.

As I draw near, the smoke wafts toward me, blurring my vision. I cough. The snap and crackle that once comforted me as the four of us sat out over the summer, roasting marshmallows together, now draws me closer to answers.

The smoke clears, and just outside the pit, items are gathered on the grass, illuminated by the glow. Something material. A rock sitting on a folded piece of paper, like the letter Logan slipped in my bathroom box before I left the apartment.

"What is this?" Mike's deep voice behind me makes me jump.

I clutch my hand to my chest and whisper, "I'm not sure."

I take a step closer and reach for the material thing. A sweater.

"Careful," Mike whispers.

I unfold the gray hoodie.

"This is Logan's—" I start, but the maroon stains stop me.

Blotches and splatters of blood—dried blood—stain the right arm and right side of the hoodie.

"That's b-b-blood," Mike stutters. "Put it down."

The reality of tonight sinks in for Mike as I drop the hoodie, picking up the scent of cologne—bergamot and cedar. Bergamot is Mike's. Cedar was Logan's. Mike hasn't seen what I have. This blood is his first tangible evidence of the horrors this night has revealed.

Whose blood is on his sweater? What has he done?

"Maybe the letter explains it," I whisper, answering my own question. I reach my shaky hand down and pick up the rock then the paper, unfolding it.

"This is—that is—" he stammers, shaking his head.

I barely hear his voice above the wind. "What?"

He squints, his gaze fixed on the paper.

Fear fills his eyes. Or is it anger?

"Just please, read the note."

My hands shake the paper so I can barely read it. I bring it closer, so afraid of what I'll find. It begins with the same scratchy kind of writing as Logan's first letter.

. . .

REMEY,

You deserve to know the truth.

Mike walks behind me, his body blocking the wind and warming my back. I think he's reading over my shoulder.

I can't handle the guilt anymore. I was seeing Marlena. Maybe you already suspected it.

Seeing Marlena? I crane my neck back. What? No... How is this possible? He was seeing her *and* accusing me of cheating? I read on, desperate for answers.

Her boyfriend got suspicious, too. She didn't want to be with him anymore, but not just because of the abuse. She wanted me. And she wouldn't let me go. So she got a knife to the heart because it was never her heart I wanted. I wanted yours.

I killed her so we could stay together, but it drove you away.

I shake my head no, looking in the direction of the fire, staring past it at a memory of Logan and me at the park. He held me close—tried to comfort me in his arms—the same arms he used to kill Marlena?

My paper shakes as I hold it tight, my knuckles white. No—he wouldn't. He couldn't.

That first night, when she used the code and knocked three times, I knew it was my chance. I knew she'd get out and try to meet her mom before the police arrived. She was already by the dumpsters by the time I caught up with her. Her boyfriend found us there, and I killed him, too. I made it look like he took his own life and hid his body a little better so it wasn't found until later.

I gasp for breath, my eyes blurry as my heart races, pounding in my ears. It can't be, but... How could he know all that? How could he have known she was meeting her mom? Her mom told us *after* she'd supposedly died. Had she confided in Logan? Had he really been seeing her?

My chest aches as I read on.

That Saturday night, I knew she was already dead, but you heard knocking. I never realized how much responsibility you'd take for her death. I never realized the guilt I'd put you through.

And after Marlena, I was scared too. I felt guilty. And then... you called me Shawn. I know it was a mistake, but it made me feel like he meant more to you than I do. Maybe that's my fault. I always hurt the people I love. And you deserve so much better.

I can't live without you. I think the best gift I can give is to let you live without me.

Logan

It can't be. Logan wouldn't...

I can't finish the thought because, if I'm being honest with myself, he could. He could have cheated. But murdering two people? I just can't believe he'd do that when he's never been violent off the rink. I've never been afraid of him before we broke up—not once.

But no one else knows those details. No one else knows about the knocking, and calling him Shawn in the park, and then the blood on his hoodie...

Stunned, I turn to Mike in shock, but he's already looking at me.

"That's a—a suicide note," he stutters. "He—he killed Marlena."

He knew Marlena? Maybe he'd heard about her murder in our building... but the way he said her name with familiarity in his inflection, like he's said it a million times... he must have known her.

"You knew her?"

He turns his attention from me, to the note, then back to me. "She—she was my sister. She was murdered. She was left in the apartment building—" He chokes on the words—he can't bear to say it. He can't say garbage, or dumpster, because that's his sister.

His...*sister*? How is that possible? Why hadn't he told me? It happened mere weeks ago. Then again, tonight was our first date, and we didn't make it past a single drink where he admitted to not knowing my name.

His glossy eyes reflect the fire back to me. "She was murdered by her boyfriend. I—I didn't know it was happening—the abuse. Nobody told me what was happening to her. I was the last to know, and by the time our mom told me—"

I wrap my arms around him, pulling him close. "I'm so sorry, Mike."

The notes of bergamot that had been associated with a nervous chemistry between us, and with the love and loyalty he'd shared with me for the people he loves, are now jarring, reminding me of the bloody hoodie on the ground between us. He'd said he'd be there in a heartbeat for the people he loves. He's been grieving her loss all this time, too.

He pulls out of my embrace. "I don't understand. How did you know her?"

"We... we lived next door." My chest aches with such intensity, I think I might be having a heart attack.

Her brother was so close all that time, in the same building, and never knew what was happening to her. He couldn't save her because he wasn't given the opportunity, but I was. She trusted me, and I failed her.

Mike pulls me into his arms. I gasp for breath. This isn't right. He doesn't realize the part I played—that I didn't act quickly enough to save her.

"Remey. My God, Remey."

"I'm sorry," I repeat, over and over. "I'm so sorry for what happened to her."

The release of my regrets is painful and cathartic at the same time, to finally apologize to someone who understands what happened. The tightness in my chest releases, leaving more room for me to breathe, and to hold him tighter.

"I tried—" I start, desperate to explain my part in Marlena's death, now that we both have Logan's confession.

"I thought—I thought it was Scott," he stammers, pulling away from me. I release him reluctantly as he reaches for the note. I hand it to him. "I can't—"

He wheezes and bends over, grasping his thighs above his knees, crumpling the letter between his hand and dress pants. He's hyperventilating—taking in sharp breaths, just like Marlena used to.

Marlena and Logan? I can't imagine it... I guess I never really knew Logan at all. I listened to him—delaying the help Marlena needed.

I rest my hand on Mike's back, choking on my tears. "Mike, I'm so sorry. Please, let's go inside. Let's wait for the police."

"I can't breathe," he says, wheezing.

"Do you have asthma?"

He shakes his head no. It's probably a panic attack.

I push him back toward the house, and he lets me guide him, wheezing along the way and gasping for breath as wind blows my loose strands of hair across my face. I open the sliding door and peer down the short hallway to the front door.

No flashing red and blue, yet.

I step inside, the glass at the bottom of my boot almost tripping me until I grab the back of the kitchen chair. I pull the seat out for Mike to sit on, and when he does, I hobble to the stove and twist the knob for the burner the kettle sits on. My legs wobble beneath me, and I lean against the oven handle for support.

Logan killed Marlena.

They were together, and he killed her so I wouldn't find out the truth.

If this is true, she really *is* dead because of me.

I've made mistakes, Rem, he'd said in his first letter. He'd been so eager to dissuade me from calling the police for Marlena Saturday night. He was almost uninterested—so insistent on doing nothing. He seemed so calm, wanting to watch a movie and ignore what was happening, but was he scared? Not exactly. He was protecting himself. Because he'd murdered her.

"Remey." Mike's deep, shaky voice reaches me from where he sits at the table. He studies the note clutched in both his hands. "Could I please have some water?"

I've carried so much guilt with no place to put it, but now, with Marlena's brother here, I can help him.

"I'm making us some tea." We could both use it. "Take deep breaths, okay? In, one, two, three. Out, one, two, three. In."

This time, he does it, and he continues on as I grab two mugs from the cabinet and two bags of Sleepytime tea to calm us. Notes of chamomile and mint waft toward me as I toss the bags in the mugs.

"Keep breathing," I call over my shoulder. "The police will be here soon."

And they'll pass Logan on their way. Will they stop, or will they keep driving like Mike, unaware that their killer is dead on the shoulder of the road?

He took my phone so I'd have to leave to get help—so I'd have to find him like that. But why? No. He didn't want me to find him. He wanted me to follow the rose petal path and find the truth. He drugged me some-how, took my phone, left the bedroom and knocked on the door to wake me, then ran off before I could catch him.

I glance over my shoulder at Mike.

"I can't believe it," Mike says, still poring over the letter. "I can't catch my breath. I don't understand how this all..."

His voice trails away as he stares at the note, entranced.

I hobble around the island and stand behind him at the table, resting a hand on his shoulder. We read together.

Remey,

You deserve to know the truth. I can't handle the guilt anymore. I was seeing Marlena. Maybe you already suspected it.

It's scratchy writing, like it was done quickly, just like the first, but is it his? I can't tell...

A knife to the heart because it was never her heart I wanted. I wanted yours.

It just doesn't sound like him. *Am I making excuses because I'm in denial?* My eyes race over the words, looking for a clue—something I've missed. But everything suddenly seems wrong. The noises, the knocking, the dead body in the road, my missing phone. A roaring fire that I didn't notice when I woke up. And... Mike showing up here in the right place—a place I don't remember telling him about—at the right time. And he's related to Marlena. Could Mike have known what Logan did to his sister somehow?

My hand slides off his shoulder, and he looks up at me. "Remey, you must be in shock. I can get the water myself—"

"No, it's fine," I tell him, returning to the stove. "It's tea. I'm making us tea."

I lift the little spoon from the sugar bowl beside the stove. It shakes with my hand as I scoop us each some.

Why aren't the police here yet?

The chair screeches along the floor, and my hand shakes, spilling some of the sugar from the spoon onto the counter.

"I've got it," I tell him, calling over my shoulder. "It's almost ready."

I can feel him moving closer, and my muscles clench. I look behind me.

He steps away from the kitchen table, toward the island countertop that separates us. "I think I should call the police again. I don't know what's taking so long, but they need to see all this. We need to get you checked out."

The thought of hearing him call the police—the fact that he suggested it—gives me a chance to breathe. To think. "Good idea. Thank you."

I'm missing something. There has to be something that makes it all make sense. I'm focused on the details of Logan's confession, but for him to have done all this... Maybe the answer lies in something Logan *didn't* say.

Mike pulls his cell phone from his pocket. As I turn back to the stove, headlights shine across the front bay window in the living room. I open my mouth to tell him they're here, but there are no red-and-blue flashing lights. No sirens.

The kettle whistles, and I startle, removing it from the stove, desperate for the quiet I need to make sure I can hear footsteps at my back. I can't explain it, but it makes me nervous. My heart races. I pour the steaming water into each mug.

In the letter, Logan said Marlena was going to leave Scott for him. If he was cheating with Marlena, why would she entrust *me* with her mom's phone number? Why wouldn't she have given it to him at another time? The letter also said it was *my* heart he wanted. Logan was dramatic like that, but what was the point in telling me it was why he stabbed Marlena in the heart? He knows how much I cared about her well-being. He knew how much hearing it had upset me tonight on the phone with him... so why would he let those be some of the last words I associate with him?

A metal jingling comes from the foyer. The front door. Someone's here.

"Remey?" a light voice calls from the front foyer.

Nicole? A nervous, excited energy blooms inside me at her voice.

Mike turns toward the entrance to the kitchen, his back facing me.

"Nicole!" I call, desperate for her to know that I'm here, and I need her.

Mike doesn't turn back to me. Instead, he walks toward the kitchen entrance.

I have to tell Nicole everything. I have to show her the letter. Logan's last words—they're all I can think about—seared in my memory. Logan's sloppy writing. *There's no easy way to tell you.*

There—for once, spelled right.

"Hey," Nic calls, her confused voice echoing down the hallway. "Whose car is that in the driveway? Oh. Hi."

14

I bring a mug of tea over to Mike and catch my first glimpse of Nicole's shocked expression.

He gives me a double take as I stop beside him, handing it to him. "Careful, it's hot."

"Oh, thanks."

I round him, rushing down the hallway, my imbalanced boots making me trip toward her. Every clenched muscle in my body wills him not to follow close behind me. Every inch away from him, every inch nearer to her, the more that frantic energy rushes through me.

The police aren't coming—no one is.

Logan didn't write that letter. He might not have killed himself—or anyone else. Mike's involvement far surpasses anything I can understand. If Mike thought Logan killed Marlena, why would he involve me like this? And who did what tonight? Was it all Logan, or all Mike? If it was a set-up, how could Mike know about the knocking, and Shawn—everything except for the misspelled "there's"? It doesn't make sense. I need more time...

I stop in front of Nicole, and my body blocks hers from Mike's view, less than twenty feet away.

Nicole's shoulders rise to a permanent shrug as she whispers, "I got your text."

She shakes her head in a micromovement, her eyes open wide, waiting for an explanation. I need to keep him feeling involved—I can't let him know I'm suspicious.

"Nicole, this is Mike." I turn to look over my shoulder. He's still standing back by the kitchen, leaning against the doorframe with his mug in both hands. "Mike was my date tonight. This is my best friend, Nicole. It's her parents' house."

I turn back to Nicole, and she stiffens, her jaw clenched. She knows the rule: we never let them know where we live before a third date.

"Nicole, the police are on their way," he says, his voice still shaky. "Remey will fill you in, I'm sure."

"The *police?*" Nicole's puzzled, concerned expression turns into one of dismay. "What happened? I got your voicemail and your text. Was it the noises?"

I frown, my gaze drifting to the floor as I try to compute. My voicemail, right, from when I was hearing noises. But I never sent a text...

Her frown mirrors mine, turning her attention to the rose petal path in the kitchen, leading to the sliding doors. "What—"

"It was Logan. Logan killed Mike's sister, Marlena," I say, then turn to Mike.

He's back at the kitchen table, sipping at the mug of tea. When he realizes I'm giving him my attention, he lowers it, still seemingly in a trance because he's not making eye contact anymore. I turn back to Nicole. I can't waste any time.

"Listen to me, okay? Logan's body is in his car, parked on the road out there."

"His body?" she mouths. Her chest and neck are turning a splotchy pink. "What the fuck?"

"Yes," I hiss, grabbing her arms and staring in her eyes. I whisper, "Hug me."

She wraps her arms around me, her comforting scent of vanilla-satsuma bringing tears to my eyes. It's the comfort I've been wanting—needing—since before she even left.

"Is he looking?" I whisper.

"He's drinking his tea, watching, yes."

"Go out to your car and call the police. Don't come inside until they get here." Nicole stiffens in my arms. "Go now. Say you'll be right back."

I release her, and she nods.

"I'm just going to my car, and I'll be right back, okay? I promise." She turns toward the door.

A scuffling noise comes from behind us. I swivel around. Mike is walking our way quickly, his shoulders back, and his furrowed brow accentuated by the light above in the middle of the foyer ceiling. I take a step away from him as he reaches the halfway point.

Nicole grabs my arm from behind.

Mike stops before me, within reach of me, clutching the note. My stomach clenches, and I brace myself, shaking Nicole off of me, pushing her arm toward the door behind my back.

He knows. He knows we're onto him.

His intense stare from below the shadow of his brow makes my heart race and keeps me frozen in fear. "I can't let you leave."

15

Nic pulls me toward the front door with her, opening it, but he grabs me. She pulls me harder, like a tug of war. He yanks back, my arms burning with pain. I reel toward him, falling against his chest. He wraps his arms around me, turning me away from Nicole and toward the kitchen. I struggle to free myself, but he's so much stronger.

"*Mike.*" I push off of him, and he lets me this time. I stumble forward as footsteps clunk behind me.

"Until the police come, I can't let you go out there by yourself." Mike's deep voice is smooth once more, as if he's trying to persuade us to trust him.

I turn around, expecting to see him in front of me, but he's through the door and grabbing a fistful of Nicole's blonde curls, yanking her backwards inside. "Remey, you have to listen to me. I'm trying to protect you."

I try to shake my head and back away as Nicole

struggles to free herself from him. He pushes her inside and closes the door behind them.

Nicole grabs her hair close to her scalp and pulls away. "Ow!"

Mike's attention is back on me, standing between us and the front door. "Logan would have done the same to you. I couldn't let it happen again. He was no good for you, Remey."

He couldn't let it happen again... He killed Logan to stop him from killing me? Logan had his faults, but he wasn't violent. He wasn't an abuser. When I found Logan sitting in his car, I leaned in to see him and opened the door that was the only thing that stood between us—even though I was scared—because in my gut, I knew he wouldn't hurt me. Mike had sliced Logan's wrists open and left him bleeding out, killing him for revenge?

Did Mike find Logan here along with the letter? Did he kill him after reading it?

I feel it in my heart—in the pit of my gut—that Mike killed him. Anger bubbles through my veins, burning at my depths as Mike stands before me. Nicole rubs at her head, her eyes glossy with tears, watching him as he inches toward me, keeping his eyes on her.

I couldn't let it happen again, he said.

I wipe my sweaty palms together, fighting against my nerves with his full attention on me. His attention, once flattering, now makes me sick.

I pull my arm out of one of the hoodie sleeves. "What did you do, Mike?"

He raises his hands, turning his attention to me with confusion as he stands directly between Nicole and me. "Don't—don't do this, Remey."

I can give Nic a chance to escape. I have his attention. I catch her eyes for a moment with a small nod. She side-steps toward the front door. She understood. My chest heaves with hope as I take a deep breath and focus my stare on Mike. He licks his lips, his hands still held out before him as I clutch the hoodie in my fists.

His face was the last thing Logan saw.

"What did you do to Logan?" I scream in his face, startling him.

I rip his sweater over my head and fling it to the floor. The motion sends my pill bottle flying from the front pocket, skittering and scraping across the tile toward him. It catches his attention.

Nicole casts the front door open. He turns and lunges for the door, reaching for her. My heart lurches. No—I won't let him lay another finger on her. I grab at his arm, clawing and grasping at the white material of his shirt, but he's faster, stronger. Mike yanks Nicole back inside and hurls her against the foyer floor. I move toward her, but he stumbles into me with momentum and we collide. I fall back from the blow, reaching my hands out through the air to catch myself, but there's nothing to grab. The back of my shoulder hits the wall first, pain throbbing through as the back of my head smashes against it. Bright white fills my eyes. Pain erupts through my head. As my vision returns, little circles of light bloom in front of Mike.

Mike turns to me, his eyes wide in shock. Nicole lies on the floor within reach of his feet, curled up on her side, facing away from us. I want to call out to her —to make sure she's okay—but I can't think straight through the pain.

"I—I didn't mean for that to happen. You have to let me explain," his normal smooth, deep voice is higher in pitch as he reaches toward me.

I flinch, taking a step back against the wall as my head throbs.

He stops, pressing his lips together and cocking his head to the side with a worried look. "I was trying to protect you, Remey."

"Your sister..." I gasp, squeezing my eyes shut, trying to block out the pain. "She died..."

"Because of Logan," he spits.

"No." I gasp, pressing my fingers to the back of my head.

I release a hiss at the searing pain, but my fingers are dry. I don't think I'm bleeding—not externally— so why does it hurt so much? Why won't it stop hurting?

"Yes." He takes a step toward me, and I slide further down the hallway, away from Nicole to gain space from him. "And Scott, and men like them. I couldn't stop him from killing her."

I'm not sure which "him" he's referring to, but before I can ask, Nicole is scrambling to her feet, her boots scuffing the tile of the front foyer. His face changes from desperation to annoyance in seconds, and he lunges at her. He grabs her arm, and I stagger toward him as she winces in pain.

I can't take it anymore—she doesn't deserve any of this. This wouldn't be happening if it weren't for me.

"Let her go!" I shout, beating my fists against his side and back.

He shakes his head and pushes me away. "Not until you listen to me."

It's not a hard push, but I stumble back, my stomach muscles clenched as I press my fingers to my temples. "I *am* listening. Just let her go. She's not a part of this. She—"

He grabs both of her arms and turns her to face me. Nicole's red-splotched neck and chest puff out toward me as her face twists in pain.

"Let her go!" I scream, my voice ripping through my own head, and I wince as it bursts in a singular echo in the foyer.

Mascara tears stain Nicole's cheeks and shine by the light above. Her red eyes stare into mine, seeming to plead with me to do something.

I'm trying, Nic. I'm so sorry.

"Let's all just sit down," Mike says from behind her, his smooth, deep voice back in a calming tone. "I can explain."

He leads her past me, toward the kitchen.

I look at the front door—mere feet away. I should run. I should leave to get help, but Nicole has her phone and I don't have a cell at all. She has her keys. I could run for the neighbours' house, but what would he do to her by the time I get back here? The blood dripping from Logan's wrists. The metallic smell from inside the car. Mike set him up so well, he made me question Logan. He's smart and he's desperate. He'll find a way to kill her and then come after me.

A hard lump forms in my throat. I can't leave her. I can't risk it.

He's terrifying, and yet, he keeps this calm demeanor. He looked genuinely shocked to see he'd hurt me. I don't think he ever planned to hurt me. This was all because of his sister. Scott hurt his sister, and he couldn't save her. He wants to be the hero.

"Please, you're holding me too tight," Nicole cries. Maybe she's noticed it, too—his savior complex. "Listen, whatever you want to tell us, we're listening."

"You're hurting her, Mike." I speak slowly, softly, in a tone I'm sure he doesn't recognize from me.

But it reminds me of Marlena's—bluebells in the breeze—and I hope it does for him, too.

"I'm sorry," he mutters, stopping halfway down the hall between the foyer and kitchen.

I walk after him slowly, each unbalanced wobble a step closer to Nicole, still wrapped tightly in his arms.

I could jump on him from behind, but he's too strong. I take another step.

He peers back over his shoulder, and his strained effort to see me is short-lived. He turns back toward the kitchen and kicks his hoodie against the wall, out of his path. "Just sit down."

I don't have my glass file anymore. Another step.

I could—

I stumble and brace myself against the wall with my palm.

The glass.

Mike turns and looks over his shoulder again and shakes his head. "I'm so sorry, Remey. I'll take a look at your head once we get you both a seat."

He turns back and walks Nicole toward the kitchen.

I lift my leg up and squat slightly, grabbing the hoodie from the floor.

"Please, just don't hurt us." Nicole's voice comes from a little further ahead, but I concentrate on using the wall for balance as I rest my boot against my other knee.

I wrap the cotton material around the shard, just like my ribbon in Logan's hand, pinching my fingers to grasp it. I tug at the green glass until it's free from my boot—all four jagged inches of it.

"I don't want to hurt anybody," Mike says.

I take ginger, stable steps toward them, the shard still clutched in the cotton material to protect my fingers. If I could get him to turn his head enough so I can stick the glass right in his eye, that could work. But if he turns his whole body, Nicole will be in the way— he could use her as a shield. I can't take the chance.

I close the distance between us before the entry to the kitchen.

I push up to stand on my toes, wrapping my arm over his shoulder, and jab the green glass at his neck. The back of his arm thrusts against me, pushing me away, and I miss... no... not completely. The shard rips through his white dress shirt and the skin of his shoulder. Warm blood stains the hoodie in my hand. He twitches, bellowing a word I can't understand as I tear it up toward his neck with all my might.

"What the hell?" he hollers, releasing Nicole with his bad arm.

Mike shakes me loose with the other, stopping me from reaching his neck, and I scramble, grasping at the shard to push it in further. He blocks me, pressing his hand to the crevice in his shoulder. His fingers hit the shard, and he releases Nicole. She stumbles forward.

I brace, ready for him to turn to me—hit me—but he pushes Nicole around the corner, down the long hallway toward the bedroom.

"No!" I scream, running after them.

I lunge at him, grasping for the glass sticking out of his shoulder. He doesn't stop, and I can't reach it. He grabs Nicole, drags her into the bedroom, and pushes the door closed in my face.

I raise my hand and the wooden door smacks against my palm, stopping it from closing completely. I barely register the jarring motion as I force it open and push past it. He's dragging her toward the bathroom, and she screams incoherently—at him or for me, I can't tell. I charge toward them, reaching out, my heart pounding in my ears.

He shoves her into the bathroom. She stumbles in, bracing herself with her hands against the far wall with the window.

"Nicole!"

Nicole twists around, pushing herself off the wall. There's a terror in her eyes I've never seen before as they lock with mine. I throw myself at the door, but it slams closed.

"Remey!" Nicole's blood-curdling scream rips through the night—through my chest. I can't lose her.

I grab the knob and pull, just as it clicks. My heart sinks. I twist at it—shake it. I pull back with all my weight, eager to rip it right out of the door. But my heart knew what my mind couldn't accept.

I'm too late.

16

"Nicole," I cry, banging on the door with my fists. "Don't you dare hurt her!"

"Let me go!" she shouts, and something clunks and thuds behind the door. He's throwing her around in there. "Don't touch me!"

My muscles flinch with each sound—each cry. I'm back at the apartment. Only this time, I'm doing everything I can to stop it, and it isn't working. He's not listening to me.

"Please!" I take a step back. "Please, Mike. I know you don't want to hurt her! You never wanted Marlena to get hurt. You just wanted to protect her. I know you're trying to protect me."

"Because you know I'm different," he calls, the desperation in his deep voice shocking me. The sounds of struggle stop. Nicole has gone silent, but I still hear her breathing—little hiccupping gasps. "I'm not like

Logan or Scott," he says. "I just need a chance to explain."

He wants us to know he's different. "This is your chance." I lower my voice to let him know I'm serious. I have to play along with him if I want him to open the door. I look over my shoulder and scan the bedroom for something—anything to help me once I get him to open this door. The thick, wooden base of the lamp on the nightstand, maybe? It's square, and the corners would hurt if I swung it at him.

But I frown when my gaze reaches the dresser. The letter and the matches—they're gone. He read Logan's letter and then he... he wrote his own. That's how he knew things he shouldn't have. But he hadn't noticed the wrong spelling of "there."

"Nicole?" I call. "You haven't hurt her, have you?"

A muffled groan comes from the other side of the door.

"She's okay. I just had to put something in her mouth so I could hear my own thoughts. And so you could hear me."

I lean against the center of the door, my palms resting on the wood, my nose almost touching it so he can hear how close I am. "I'm listening, Mike."

"My mom told me the truth about Scott the Saturday before Marlena's body was discovered—how he'd been hurting her. At first, I couldn't believe it. He had a great job. He took care of her, provided for her. I was sure I'd have known if something bad was happening." *Except, if the neighbour was right, Scott had lost his job. Did they lie to her family about it?* "So I told her he wasn't that kind of man… That's when my mom told me about the plan. The knocking. That's when I… understood." His somber voice leads me to think he resigned himself to revenge right then. "I'd thought Marlena and I were drifting apart; we went weeks without seeing each other. But no, it was him, taking her phone, isolating her so that she had to resort to knocking on the wall for help." Anger rises in his inflection as he races through the explanation. "All that time, and I had no idea. Until Marlena didn't show up. That's when Mom went to you. Then, she came to me."

Telling Mike seems like a last resort. Maybe she was afraid of what he'd do, but with Marlena missing, she probably felt like she had no choice.

"My mom said Marlena trusted you," he said. "You all had an arrangement—a pact. I took my mom's spare and went to their apartment Saturday night. No one was home, but all of her things were there. Do you know what else I found? You and your boyfriend. I heard you on the other side of the wall, watching a movie."

He stood behind that wall, listening to us.

I clench my cold fingers into fists at my sides. "You're the one who knocked the second night."

Logan had been wrong. I wasn't hearing things. I was never crazy.

Mike was there—testing us. And that night, when no one knew Marlena was already dead, we failed.

17

"I had to know if you'd hold up your end of the arrangement." There's a pause and a shuffling across the floor. *What is he doing in there?* "I had to figure out what happened Friday night—why Marlena never met Mom. I heard Logan try to stop you from calling her." At the mention of his name, venom seeps from Mike's voice and the scuffling turns into footsteps, neither closer nor further. He must be pacing. "He tried to stop you from calling the police. He tried to gaslight you into believing there hadn't even been any knocking. I heard the whole thing."

Like you're trying to gaslight me into believing they were seeing each other. That Logan killed your sister when he didn't? She was already dead—Scott killed her.

Logan and I both thought we were doing the right thing. He wasn't cheating. He wasn't a killer. I straighten off the door, my chest heaving. Logan and I didn't agree about how it was handled, and I should

have listened to my own gut, but Logan was as inno-
cent as I was.

But Mike doesn't want to hear that. He wants me to
know that he's different. And I still don't understand...

"So, you heard us go to the apartment, then. We
went to check and see if Marlena was okay. You were in
there." I lean in toward the door. "You *know we tried*."

"*You* tried! He didn't. You didn't even call the police.
She could have been in there, getting strangled to
death, and you just knocked and left. Logan left her for
dead!"

"She was already dead that night," I whimper.
Logan had told me the truth tonight on our last phone
call. That's the last time I'll ever talk to him—all
because Mike thought he heard everything. He thinks
he knows the efforts we made—but he doesn't. "When
we went back to our apartment, I called the police," I
shout, pounding my fist against the door. "I did it,
despite the fact Logan tried to warn me that we'd get in
trouble if no one was home. I called." I step away from
the door. "And I should have done it sooner." I wrap
my arms across my chest, over my cool, satin pajama
top. It soothes me as I take a deep, shuddering breath.
"I was too late..."

"*I* was too late." His voice is lower, softer. *Is he
further away from the door?* "We were all too late, but
Logan... if he'd have been any sort of man, he'd have
gone over there and stopped Scott from killing my
sister!"

It transports me back to the apartment, back to the

nights of the yelling, and crying, and banging. I stare at the door, my chest heaving, my nails digging into my palms. I want to defend Logan, but the pointed pain brings me back into the moment. Marlena's gone, and so is Logan, but I have to save Nicole.

I press my ear against the door. Is he close to the door, too, or is he with Nicole? Is he hurting her? Shivers run down my back. I take a deep breath and inch closer to the crack of the door.

"I'm sorry." I keep my voice soft again, like Marlena's. I can't lose it on him again until we're safe. "I'm so sorry Scott killed her."

Nothing. It's so quiet on the other side.

"Mike?" I call gently. "I know you loved Marlena. I know you would have done anything for her because you're a good man."

"She doesn't get another chance," he says straight away, closer to the door. "But you did. You had a chance to leave him before he hurt you... and you didn't. That's why I was going to end his life that day in the park. But he didn't look the same as when I saw him through the peephole in Marlena's door, and you called him the wrong name. So I swerved."

The cold chill of adrenaline takes hold of my body.

Logan cut all his curly hair off at the end of his hockey season. The buzz cut and a name—Shawn. That's what saved him that day, but it didn't stop Mike from operating under his assumptions and delusions. It didn't stop him from finding Logan again and cutting his life short. He inserted himself into my life—called me "Neighbour" when he *knew* my name.

Does Mike even live in that building?

"You called him by your ex's name, and he *still* wanted you back. He still wouldn't leave you alone. He was going to hound you and stalk you until you gave up or—or he lost it and killed you. I had to make sure it didn't happen again."

He's delusional. He won't hear what he doesn't want to believe. He thinks he saved me from Logan. He's trying to make up for not being able to save Marlena.

"Please," I gasp, "just let me in. I understand now. I know you were just trying to protect me. And Nicole is on your side! She's been trying to get me to leave Logan for months. She wanted me to burn that letter. You saw the matches beside it. But I couldn't let go of the past. You both helped me—" I clear my throat, so my voice won't shake with visions of Logan's dead body in his car, soaked with blood. Had Mike been the one to write "I'm sorry" in his blood? My stomach churns and heaves as I choke out my words. "You've both taken such good care of me." *Let her go, Mike. Be a hero.*

The knob wiggles. His hand must be on it. He wants to let me in. I stare at the knob as hope fills my lungs with each breath I take. It's working. This has to work.

I lean against the door, as close as I can get to the opening crack. "You set it up perfectly, Mike—you saved me. And the police will see exactly what we need them to. That Logan was dangerous. That he was after me. You and Nicole saw it when I couldn't."

The knob twists. I want to burst inside, but I steady myself and take one step back. I need to wait for the right moment. The door creaks open. His misty eyes focus on me, but he clenches the knob in his bloody hand, as if he might change his mind. Bright red soaks the shoulder of his dress shirt, and streaks of blood lead from his wound, meeting his pants where his shirt is tucked in. The piece of jagged green glass still protrudes from his shoulder.

"It's not as bad as it looks," he whispers, stepping aside.

Nicole sits behind him to my left, her back slumped against the tub beside my boxes with her knees to her chest and a washcloth balled up in her open mouth. Her wide, red eyes find mine. Desperate. Scared. There's only one way out of this.

I wrap my arms around Mike's waist and rest my cheek against his chest. He stiffens at first, and then releases the knob, wrapping his arms around my waist with a short grunt of pain. His shoulder must hurt when he uses his arm. That's something. I'll use any advantage I can get.

I press Logan's killer's body against mine, shaking with disgust. I keep my lips pressed together to muffle my sobs and to stop myself from being sick, but the bergamot sends me over the edge. A deep cry escapes my lips, and he holds me tighter.

I keep my cheek pressed to his chest as I push

across it, over the cold, wet blood, and peek past his injured shoulder. Nicole sits, watching us with wide eyes. I give her a look—a solemn promise in my stare.

I will get us out of here.

Beside her, Logan's cologne rests on top of my nail polish in the box. Mike used the woods-scented cologne on the bloody hoodie to make me associate it with Logan. Sneaky—but not enough to cover his own scent. Was the hoodie even his? He's cunning—dangerous—and if I do something to lose his trust, I'm not sure he'll ever believe me again.

"You saved me," I whisper, pulling away. I nod to Nicole. "You saved *us*."

He licks his lips, reaching his hand toward mine until his bloody fingers graze my palm. "I didn't hurt her. I needed you to hear me." He turns to Nicole. "I'm so sorry."

"I know." I gently hold his hand in mine, swallowing at the lump in my throat and forcing myself to smile. "We understand now. Could you take that out of her mouth and untie her, please?"

He squints down at me. "I think we need to leave it, and when the police come, we'll tell them Logan did it to her."

Nicole shakes her head back and forth slowly, once, looking at me.

"She has to go along with the plan," Mike whispers to me.

"She will," I promise, slipping my hand out of his. I reach for his shoulder where a little of the green shard still protrudes from his skin. He flinches but doesn't budge. "I'm going to need to take a look at this. I'm so sorry I hurt you. I didn't understand."

"It's okay." He takes my hand away from his shoulder and presses it against his chest, wincing. "Like I said, worse than it looks. The paramedics will take care of it."

Disappointment sinks down to my stomach, but I stick to the plan.

I step toward Nicole.

He follows me. "I don't think that's a good idea."

Instead of stopping, I gently pull his hand along with me. He needs to be the one in control. He needs to be the one who helps us—who saves us.

"We really should take that out of her mouth. Please? She'll probably thank you for finally removing Logan from my life for good. She knew he was bad. I couldn't see it. I didn't want to." My eyes scan the room. They land on the curling iron. I wish I hadn't turned that thing off earlier. Why had he plugged it back in? Was I supposed to think that was something Logan did to freak me out?

"Sometimes, you just don't want to believe the worst in people. My sister didn't see how bad Scott was, either," he says, sighing, releasing my hand. He bends over and pulls the washcloth out of her mouth with his good hand. "Until it was too late."

Nicole coughs and licks her lips, glancing from me to him.

Please, Nicole. Please go along with him until the police arrive. We're so close.

"Thank you," she says, her scratchy voice barely concealing her revulsion.

He nods and stands up straight.

Nicole rests her hand on the flat outer ledge of the tub and shifts to one knee, lifting the other leg. I hope she'll keep herself small—non-threatening. If we can just convince him we're on his side and appreciative of what he's done, he'll call the police for us like he was about to do before Nicole came.

Mike reaches his hand down to help her up, and she hesitates. Her eyes flash with anger, widening at me and then squinting at him. She's going to do something. She's trying to give me a signal to get ready—I feel it in my gut.

I open my eyes wide and shake my head ever so slightly. *No, Nicole, no.* She uses his hand to stand and stumbles back a bit. He steadies her, reaching out for her, and winces as she takes a step in front of him, out of his grasp. As she releases his hand, she raises her arms in front of her and bends to the side. She charges forward, knocking her shoulder against his chest, pushing him toward the tub.

18

M ike latches onto Nicole's jacket and twists, shoving her down instead, into the tub. She falls onto her back with a thud and a gasp, her knees bent over the ledge, her legs dangling off the side. I grab at him, trying to pull him away. I can't see her face from behind him, but I hear her gasping for breath. I push against his arm enough for Nicole to come into view, lying on the bottom of the tub. He's fallen to his knees by the side of the tub and grabs her hands. She bursts into tears, her face bright red. While she writhes in pain, he has her wrists locked in seconds; her skin is white around his grip. Her sobs of pain echo through the bathroom.

Mike holds her down, grunting in pain. "Ah, shit. I'm sorry, Remey! You saw what she tried to do! She doesn't understand."

"Let her go!" I shout, then round his body to his right side with his bad arm. He leans back, pushing his body between Nicole and me. I reach for his shoulder, for the glass, "She's hurt! You need to—"

He lifts his elbow to block my hand and connects with my nose. I blink back the tears and shooting pain, stumbling back, still reaching out in front of me. My nose burns as blood trickles from it. The metallic smell becomes taste as it drips to my lips and off my chin. I'm still reaching out ahead—reaching out to save her through my blurry vision. The water gushes on, smattering against the bottom of the tub, and my head throbs with the echoing noise washing out the others. Nicole's cries turn into gagging, gurgling noises. I don't have to see to know what's going on, but as my vision returns and I wipe the blood from my lips, the scene unfolds before me.

The struggle feels like it's happening in another place, to someone else. Nicole whacks at his face with her hands and kicks her legs, but it causes her to slip into the tub further with each kick, until her whole body's trapped inside the porcelain.

"Mike." My voice sounds strangely calm, unlike my own. I'm bursting with pain, screaming on the inside for him to stop. I just want it to stop.

"Please." Blood sprays from my mouth, speckling the white bath mat.

"We'll have to say he killed her, too," he says, focusing only on Nicole, holding her face under the flowing water. She claws desperately at his face.

"Stop this, Mike. Just come with me." I grab onto

his arm and try to pull him away from her. "I'll go wherever you want."

He doesn't move. Not with Nicole's nails scratching at his face. Not at my request. I can't reason with him anymore. I have to help her.

I reach into the tub and grab Nicole's wet coat, catching my grip around her arms, trying to pull her toward me and away from the water. Her face tilts to the side and she gasps for breath, grasping for me. I find strength from that glimmer of hope and pull her head out from directly beneath the running tap. She grabs hold of my arms, but he pulls her away, back under. He's too strong. Water from the tap beats down on her face, into her mouth. I keep a hold of her, hoping she can feel me. That she knows I'm right here with her. If I let her go—lose momentum—he'll drown her. I don't know how much longer she has left.

My arm muscles burn, and the more I pull, the more I tire. I'm not strong enough to pull her out. I'm not strong enough to pull him off of her. Nicole was right. She's been right the whole time.

I have to let go.

19

Consumed with guilt and dizzy with so much pain in my head, I release my best friend into Mike's control. I stumble back from the tub. My curling iron still rests on the counter. No red light. No heat. No other choice.

In one swipe, I grab the handle. It presses into the burned spot of flesh on my palm, but the pain barely registers with the ache of my nose and the back of my head throbbing. I whip back around, running my other hand along the length of the smooth, black cord, edging toward the tub—toward Mike. Nicole's arms and legs are still—no longer struggling. Before my eyes, her body convulses. She doesn't have much time left. The energy to stop him bursts beneath my flesh, propelling me forward.

I bring the cord in front of him, wrapping it around his neck.

"Remey?" He finally snaps out of his fixation on

Nicole, turning his head toward me. His eyes widen and his jaw drops as he takes in the sight of my face. The blood. I lick my lips. The metallic taste strengthens with my resolve. "What are you—"

I cross the cord behind his head and press the barrel to his face, feeling for the slightly concave slope of his eye. He finally releases Nicole. I knock his glasses off and push the tip of the barrel into his eye. He hollers in pain, and I fall back, dropping to the floor. I take him with me.

The back of my head collides with the tile and blinding, all-encompassing pain sears through my mind. His thick-framed glasses crunch beneath us. Mike's upper body writhes on top of the lower half of mine, the back of his head pressed against my stomach. I barely feel the compression. My head throbs as I listen for Nicole—waiting for her to get out of the tub. To help me.

Water smatters against the porcelain. Mike's boots scuffle and screech against the tile as he kicks, reaching into the air above, trying to pull himself off of me. I let the iron fall from my hand and grab the cord, crossing them and leaning back.

"Nicole," I gasp, but I barely make a sound as I strain to keep the tension.

The dark spots in my vision flash on and off as he struggles on top of me, trying to roll on his side, reaching his arms up at me. No, not at me—at his neck. He's pushing his fingers beneath the cord.

"Nicole, get up," I wheeze.

Why isn't she getting up?

"Nicole!" I gasp, my chest heaving.

My words feel futile.

No. This isn't over. This isn't the end.

My heart pounds in my ears. He's prying his fingers beneath the cord. I'm losing tension as he struggles. *I can't... let him... win.* I pull back with all my weight, balanced against the tension of the cord against his neck and inhale, staring up at the edge of the tub and waiting for any sign from Nicole. Once he stops moving, I can get to her. I can help her.

"Rem," Mike huffs, his hands prying at the cord.

Whether he said the short version of my name because he feels close to me or because he can't choke out the rest, it lights a fire of anger in me.

I shouldn't have let her go.

"I can't—" he sputters.

His legs still kick, but Nicole's don't. He still gasps for breath, but Nicole doesn't. He fights for his life because he still has a chance. Nicole still has a chance if I can just make him stop. No more lies or false realities where he's convinced himself he's the hero. Only the painful truth of what he's done.

"You knocked... you thought... we failed her," I wheeze. "But I called the police. You didn't... hear me... you feel... like you failed her..."

He groans something, still pulling at the cord, but his movements lack the strength he started with.

"You killed Logan... to make yourself... feel better... You didn't save me... I wasn't... a victim."

His hands slowly fall away from the cord.

"You're... getting tired, hmm?" I grunt. "All the sleeping pills... I crushed up into your tea... are finally kicking in."

He releases a hiss of breath that rattles at the end.

"*That*... is who you are," I whisper in his ear, panting, staring at the lip of the tub where my best friend lies out of my sight. I release the cord and grab the shard of glass between my thumb and index finger. "You're... not a hero. You're a killer."

I rip the glass out of his shoulder and blood spurts from the wound onto my fingers, the white tile, all over both of us. His body wiggles from side to side before it falls limp against my lower half, his head resting on my stomach. I want to wait to make sure he's not getting back up, but I can't take another second away from her. I roll his head off of me, struggling to scoot out from under him. My pulse pounds in my ears as I crawl to the tub. I scramble to my knees and lean over the top edge, my back aching as I twist the faucet off. My head spins as I lean over. So much pressure in my head... my nose...

Nicole is lying against the bottom on her back, soaking wet in a shallow puddle. Her eyes are closed— not squeezed shut, but peaceful. *No, please no. I can't lose her.* I grab her and try to pull her up, but I can barely lift her off the bottom. My fingers slip off her coat. Her body splashes back against the puddle of water beneath her.

I slide my hands beneath her arm on the far side

and press my palms against her cold, wet back. *She needs me. I need her.* With all my strength and weight, I pull her onto her side with a guttural cry.

She chokes on water, spitting it out, and opens her eyes.

"Nicole!"

She gasps for air at the same time Mike draws in a raspy breath of air behind me. I turn to see the blood drenching the front of his shirt. He presses his hand against his wound, blood spilling over his fingers.

"Remey," Nicole gasps, her arms reaching out for me as her pale face turns to mine in horror.

"Nicole." I wrap my arms around her, pulling her up to sit.

I thought you were gone, I want to say, but I can't speak. Mike gasps for breath behind me. It's not over. I push off my knees and pull Nicole up with me. Wet clothes stick to her shivering body, and as she steps out of the tub, she keeps her eyes on Mike.

"Remey." She leans against the wall beside the tub and nods toward him, her chest still heaving.

I turn to the man who killed Logan—who almost killed my best friend. His right eye is bloodshot—the one I pressed the curling iron into. He pulls his bloody hand away from his shoulder and puts both arms on the floor behind him. He scrambles backwards, away from us and toward the counter cabinets, painting the white tile with a thick, crimson streak.

I take Nicole's arm, and with my support, we walk toward him. We clear the crumpled, blood-spattered bath mat. Nicole's wet clothes drip onto the tile. Mike slumps against the cabinet, pushing his hand to his shoulder.

"I did... what I had to do," he chokes out, blinking. His puffy eye is starting to swell shut.

I don't know how he's still awake—still alive—but we can't underestimate him.

"You're safe now," he mutters, his eyes barely open.

"You must be so tired," I say in a soft, gentle tone. "The way you're blinking, your eyelids must feel *so heavy*. I know that feeling, and you can't fight it."

"All that blood," Nicole whispers slowly, feigning the same concern as we follow the smeared trail of blood across the tile.

Like the rose petal path he left for me. I take my own path, now.

I guide Nicole toward the door, and she hobbles after me. She doesn't look at him.

Closing the door behind us, she stops at the armchair in the corner of the room. "I'll call the police."

I join her, and we lift the chair, my back aching as we pull it in front of the bathroom door together to block him in. "I'll stay here... to make sure..."

We summon our combined strength and wedge it as close to the door as we can.

Nicole nods, and I grab her hand. We exchange a look that takes all of one second.

A signal or a look can convey so much more than words because it's left to the interpretation of the individuals sharing it. Sometimes, it's well-defined, like the signal people give to each other when they want to leave a social gathering. Sometimes, it holds more meaning to one than the other could ever imagine, like an agreement to call for help. Sometimes, it's a spontaneous moment shared between two people.

To me, this look means we're grateful. For each other, and to be alive.

Nicole hobbles to the door, holding her back, and disappears down the hallway. I grab the lamp from the nightstand and remove the shade. I flip it over, getting a grip on the wooden post. Shaking with adrenaline, I return to the chair and stop before it, watching the washroom door for whatever comes next.

For Mike to call to me—to try to convince me that he saved me. Or for a noise that tells me he's trying to escape. For a banging on the door.

For knocking.

But there is only silence.

20

ONE WEEK LATER

The fire in the backyard crackles as I approach the two empty lawn chairs. Nicole's parents came back a few days ago, ending their trip early to be with her. They've graciously allowed me to stay in their home until the end of the month, when I'll be moving into a basement apartment I was lucky enough to find close to Nic's house.

Crickets chirp around me above the sound of the crackles and snaps. I take a deep breath of the smoky, evening air.

Nic and I decided to spend one last night together at her parents' house. She's been helping me heal, physically and emotionally. We went to the hospital together, and although she couldn't be with me while I had my CT scan, she was there when I got the results that there'd been no internal bleeding. My nose, however, was broken. Nicole was with me when they manually realigned it, too.

"Coming," Nicole calls from behind me.

I glance over my shoulder as she approaches with a wine glass in each hand—red.

My letter to Logan is tucked beneath my arm with a throw blanket for us. My new therapist suggested writing to him and setting it free, like a message in a bottle. Since Logan's first letter to me was real, and Mike burned it right here in this fire, it feels like I'm setting his memory to rest here with my truth.

Even after Mike used the fire—used this house—to set Logan up to take the fall for everything, he didn't taint it for us. He couldn't.

Mike was arrested and charged with Scott's and Logan's murders, and I slept through the night in Nicole's parents' bed without the need for sleeping pills. Which is good, because that filled prescription ended up in evidence.

We take our seats, and I lay the blanket out over us. She extends my glass to me, but I hold up the letter, and she brings it back to her lap.

"I think I'm ready."

She nods. "Would you read it to me?"

I swallow over the lump in my throat, recalling the last time I heard Logan's voice on the phone during my date with Mike. He was trying to bring me peace. He was trying to help me, even if he had ulterior motives about reuniting.

Mike was right about a few things. Logan had followed me from the old apartment to Nicole's parents' place. He'd followed me to our date and called me from the parking lot. He hadn't followed me back home, though. While I went to the pharmacy, Logan hadn't realized I had that stop to make, so he'd gone straight to the McCowns' himself. And Mike had followed him.

The police believe Logan had been parked on the road when I'd driven past, returning home, but I'd been so preoccupied by Logan's news about when Marlena died, I hadn't seen the car in the dark. They're not sure if Logan was already dead at that point. The ME's report isn't in yet, but I'm not waiting on that news. I don't want to know whether I could have saved him or not while he bled out in his car, and that isn't how I want to think of Logan. I want to remember him when he was full of life, flaws and all.

And that bathroom stall wasn't the last I heard from Logan, either—not really.

In fact, Nicole had been the last to hear from him. Once she got out of the movie theatre with her date, before she'd even listened to my voice message from that night, she saw a text I'd sent from my phone—only it was Logan who'd sent it.

While I was fast asleep from the drugs Mike had slipped into my Mule at the restaurant, Mike had set Logan up in his car. He'd smashed my cell phone, slit Logan's wrists, and placed my phone in his hand once he thought he was dead and gone.

But the phone wasn't dead.

Neither was Logan.

Once Mike left, Logan, unable to speak, had texted Nicole.

Help Rem

That's all he'd been able to type, and he'd sent it before it ran out of battery power. It was the reason Nicole had left her date straight away. That text might be the reason I'm alive.

One thing I may never know is whether the words "I'm sorry" written on the car window were Mike's attempt to fake Logan's suicide, or if Logan had really written it. I won't know who brought those extra roses, either. Mike refuses to say.

I tug the blanket closer on my lap and hold the letter up in front of me, the light from the little fire glowing through.

"*I'm sorry, Logan.*" The words catch in my throat, and I clear it once more before continuing. "*I never meant to put you in danger, and I know you were trying to protect me in the end. Thank you for everything you did for me, and for loving me to the capacity with which you could love.*"

I sniffle, catching Nic nodding her head yes out of the corner of my eye. It's one of the realizations I came to with my therapist. Logan really did care about me, but like me, there was so much he couldn't express about how he felt—so much I'll never know. A lump forms in my throat, and I clear it, continuing.

"*We both made some of the same mistakes. Neither of us believed in me or trusted me fully. Neither of us could let go. I wouldn't have been able to grow if I hadn't left you.*"

Tears burn my eyes, and my breath catches in my throat. The fact that it's true doesn't make it any less painful to say, but I'm giving us both what we deserve, finally. I'm telling him how I feel. "*While you were here on earth, I couldn't fully let you go because I didn't want the end to take away the meaning of our time together. I realize now, it can't, and you can let go of what doesn't serve you to make room for what will.*

With this letter, I'm letting go of the pain." I inhale a deep breath of the smoky fire before me. "*I'm releasing the guilt.*" I exhale, freeing the weight in my chest. "*I'm wishing you peace, Logan. With love, Rem.*"

I wipe the tears beneath my eyes and on my hot cheeks with the back of my hand, my nose tingling with the lingering pain, reminding me of my black eyes. I turn to Nicole, her tear-soaked cheeks glistening by the firelight. She squeezes my hand. I take a deep breath, standing, letting my half of the blanket fall off my legs to the ground. I step over it, toward the fire.

Wishing you peace.

I release the message into the fire and focus my gaze on the crackling sparkle of lights, flying toward the sky. I imagine they're taking the message to him. I tilt my head back, looking up at the starry sky as I remember Logan's words in his letter.

I would have obsessed over what we could have done differently if I believed it would help at all, but I know it won't.

"Come on back here," Nicole says, clearing her

throat of the emotion that seems to be stuck in mine, too. "We have to keep each other warm."

I rejoin her, taking the chair beside where she sits under her half of the blanket. This time when she offers the wine glass, I take it. "Thank you."

Nicole takes a sip. "Of course. There's still half the bottle left inside—"

"No, I mean thank you for everything you did to save me."

She runs her fingers over the edge of her side of the blanket. "I knew you needed help. As soon as I saw a strange man in the house, and you told me it was your date, I knew something was wrong about him. You've never broken the three-date rule."

"I shouldn't have been dating again so soon at all..."

Nicole picks at the blanket. "Easy to say that in hindsight, but I'd have said yes to Mike, too. He was there for you shortly after you broke up with Logan— albeit, he had just tried to run him over. He waited for the right time to ask you out. Hell, he didn't even live in the building, but he went out of his way to run into you any chance he could. It would have seemed like good timing to me, too."

The way he set it all up still hurts—that I couldn't see through him. His own sister had known he was unstable, and she'd tried to keep him at arm's length. Their mom did, too. That's why she only told Mike about Marlena when she went missing.

I tuck my hair behind my ear and lean back in my chair. "You know, he said he first saw me when he went to visit his sister months before her death. Apparently, Marlena told him she thought I had kind eyes. That was part of his police statement... once he could speak again."

Nicole absentmindedly brushes her fingers against the blanket, starting into the fire. "It's hard to wrap my mind around how someone could do this."

I nod, still thinking about his words. "Marlena told me the same thing, too, when she asked for my help." I take a sip of the red wine, the tannins coating my tongue, then I swirl it around in the glass. "She said I had kind eyes. Her mom told the police I'd done everything I could to help Marlena—that I'd put myself in danger for her."

She crosses one leg over the other. "It's normal to wonder if we could have done more."

I nod and take another sip of wine as the flames begin to die off.

"I've been thinking about her a lot."

Nicole shifts in her seat to face me. "Marlena?"

"Her mom. One of her children was murdered, and the other is a murderer. She tried to protect them both, but now, the police say she's cooperating with them on the charges against Mike. He killed to avenge her daughter once, but with Logan, the cops think he was playing it all out again. Trying to be there for his sister in some way, through being there for me. I thought maybe she'd try to protect the only child she has left."

"But she isn't."

"No, because he still sees himself as a hero, and it disturbs her." I release a deep sigh.

Nicole lets out a huff of air and pulls her hands out from beneath the blanket, tugging it higher against her chest. "Me too. That night, in the bathroom..." Her voice breaks.

I reach for her hand and hold it. Her warm skin tingles against my numb fingers. She takes a long drink from her glass and shakes her head as she swallows. Tears slide down her cheeks again. She presses her lips together, casting a glassy look of pain toward me. There's a vulnerability there that still haunts me after witnessing the torture she went through and how close she came to death.

"I'm sorry you were there," I whisper. "And also, I'm so thankful you came."

"I know," she whispers, letting go of my hand to wipe beneath her eyes. "I just don't want to think about what could have happened if you hadn't snuck your sleeping pills in his tea."

When I read that second note, I didn't understand the danger, but I felt it. When Mike turned to watch Nicole down the hallway, I used the weight of the mug to crush up some of my pills and slipped them in his tea. I wasn't sure how or why, but I knew I wasn't safe with him. I'd never have said that on our date—I'd been charmed by him. But things changed quickly, as they so often do.

Even he was charmed by Scott, for a time. So much

so, he couldn't believe what had been done in the dark to his sister.

I'd always taken Marlena's danger and pain seriously, but I hadn't done the same for myself.

I don't hear the knocking anymore. Knowing the truth freed me in a way I hadn't thought possible, and I couldn't fully accept it until my first moment of quiet to myself.

I'll always listen to my gut, Marlena. I promise never to abandon myself again.

Little flames flicker on the last of the branches from the fire, the ember's glow rolling in magical waves beneath them.

Next month, after I move, I think I'll start journaling about this like my therapist suggested. Maybe I'll be ready to sit with my emotions and just feel them. Until then, I'll sit with Nicole. She knows all my secrets now, and she accepts me for who I am. She hasn't judged me for a single thing that I've done, even after I unknowingly dragged her into all this. We've abided by the rules we set in our friendship to keep each other safe, and I'll never take those efforts for granted again.

"I'm getting cold." Nicole nods to the fire. "Want to put it out and go inside? Maybe watch a movie?"

I press my glass to my lips and drain the rest of the wine. I swallow it, wishing the pain we'd experienced could disappear as easily.

"Sounds good." I lick the remnants from the corners of my mouth. "What do you want to watch?"

We both break into small, knowing smiles and pull

off the blanket. Exposed to the cold night air, a chill runs down my back. I shiver, eager for the warmth of the house and the cozy set-up we'll create to enjoy a favourite like we always have.

I hand my glass to her and gather up the blanket under my arm, hugging it against my side.

Nicole grins, holding up our glasses. "Shall we switch to white?"

"Let's."

She wraps her arm through mine, and we squeeze them together, shoulder to shoulder.

I'm learning the power of letting go, but some things... some things, I'll always fight to hold on to.

THANK you for reading *Knock Three Times*. If you enjoyed the story, don't miss Emerald O'Brien's psychological suspense standalone novels...

I Heard You Scream

Five can keep a secret if four are dead.

We Don't Leave

Who can you trust when you can't believe your own eyes?

The Waking Place

Givers must set limits, for takers have none.

Follow *Her Home*

She's desperate to leave the past behind her. But fear has a way of following.

What She Found

It was supposed to be the perfect getaway, but a knock at the door could ruin their lives.

She can't trust her
own eyes.

Givers must set limits,
for takers have none.

Five can keep a
secret
if four are dead.

She's desperate to
leave the past
behind but fear has
a way of following.

ALSO BY EMERALD O'BRIEN

Don't miss these suspenseful and unpredictable reads by
Emerald O'Brien

Standalone Novels:

I Heard You Scream

We Don't Leave

Follow Her Home

The Waking Place

What She Found

The Knox and Sheppard 5 Book Mystery Series:

The Girls Across the Bay (Book One)

Wrong Angle (Book One Point Five, free in Emerald's
newsletter)

The Secrets They Keep (Book Two)

The Lies You Told (Book Three)

The One Who Watches (Book Four)

The Sisters of Tall Pines (Book Five)

The Locke Industries Series:

The Assistant's Secret

The Nanny's Secret by best-selling author, Kiersten Modglin

YOUR FREE EBOOK

Emerald would love to offer you a free ebook along with updates on her new releases.

Subscribe to her newsletter today on
emeraldobrien.com

ACKNOWLEDGMENTS

Thank you to my beta readers, Kiersten Modglin, Meghan O'Flynn, and Shyla O'Brien. You helped me bring the story in my heart and mind to life on the page. I appreciate your encouragement, new ideas, understanding, and enthusiasm. Thank you for reflecting the story back to me with fresh eyes, your unique perspectives, and with such care that I'm so grateful to have received.

To Sarah at Three Owls Editing, thank you for your editing services and insightful feedback. I'm so grateful for your help.

Thank you to my colleagues in the book community for your support, encouragement, and sharing your knowledge with me. I'm proud to call you my friends.

For the continued support of my family and friends, I am forever grateful, and I love you all. Each and every person in my life who has supported me and my writing career hold a special place in my heart.

Thank you to my true-blue readers, review team, and newsletter subscribers. Your company on this journey has been a pleasure.

ABOUT THE AUTHOR

Emerald O'Brien was born and raised just east of Toronto, Ontario. She graduated from her Television Broadcasting and Communications Media program at Mohawk College in Hamilton, Ontario.

As the author of unpredictable stories packed with suspense, Emerald enjoys connecting with her readers who are passionate about joining characters as they solve mysteries and take exciting adventures between the pages of great books.

To find out more, visit Emerald on her website: emeraldobrien.com

If you enjoyed Emerald's work, please share your experience by leaving a review where you purchased the story.

Subscribe to her newsletter for a free ebook, exclusive content, and information about current and upcoming works.